THE MAN WHO CANNOT BE KILLED

The Man Who Cannot Be Killed

a Catholic Worker mystery

WARNING - STOP!
NO TRESPASSING

THIS IS A HARD HAT JOB SITE

Scott Schaeffer-Duffy

illustrated by Aiden Duffy

Haley's
Athol, Massachusetts

Haley's
488 South Main Street
Athol, MA 01331
haley.antique@verizon.net
978.249.9400

Cover illustration by Aiden Duffy:
Notre Dame Church, Worcester, during demolition

Copy edited by Ellen Woodbury.

Proof read by Richard Bruno.

International Standard Book Number: 978-1-948380-09-6

for my marathon training partner, Karen Pajer

May she never doubt her or my potential.

The reason I put everyone here naked ... I wasn't trying to be cute.
It's just that with clothes there's right away pockets,
and pockets, you gotta put something in 'em.
Trust me, like it says on the money.

-George Burns as God in the movie *Oh, God*

God is a comedian playing to an audience
that is too afraid to laugh.

—Voltaire

contents

contents (continued)

illustrations by Aiden Duffy and photos

ninety percent factual
a preface by Scott Schaeffer-Duffy

The contents of this book are ninety percent factual and ten percent fictional. After reading the first third, my son Aiden warned that readers would presume the exact opposite, but I assure you of the accuracy of my ratio, however skeptical you may be.

Even though I must admit that some of what follows is fiction, I nonetheless attest to my belief that *all* of it is true. Facts and truth differ markedly. The former rests on the empirical, while the latter involves complexity, so much so that even Pontius Pilate asks, "What is truth?"

In an age of what Steven Colbert calls "truthiness," we may not be able to know, but we still have the opportunity to believe.

Monday, April 16, 2018

I forgot to put my pants on again this morning.

You would think pants would be hard to overlook, especially on a cold April morning, but when I'm preoccupied, I accomplish tasks of the moment by auto-pilot or not at all. Thank our merciful Savior, I realized the need to put something on over my jockey shorts before a passerby or police officer pointed out my omission. Although I've heard some locales do not find skimpy dress remarkable, Worcester, Massachusetts, does not qualify as one of those places. Hereabouts, narrow parameters prevail for proper attire. You can march to a different drummer in many ways but are expected to do so wearing pants.

I don't see why the high-tech geniuses haven't come up with more reminder apps. Were it not for the beeping noise in my car, I'd have left my keys in the ignition, forgotten to put the vehicle in park, and walked away oblivious to the fact that my Prius transformed into a self-driving car. I guess Alexa comes closest to the gentleman's gentleman of bygone days. Unfortunately, I don't have Alexa to look out for me. I don't even have a cell phone or blog. I don't tweet. I don't use Instagram. I'm not on Facebook. I write letters by hand with a thing called a pen. I put them in an envelope to which I affix a stamp, and I thank Ben Franklin when an employee of the postal service sees to it that my missives reach their destinations. If I didn't have email, some people would have long ago assumed I died or never existed at all.

All things considered, I'm just about the least technologically competent twenty-first-century American I know, hardly the kind of dude you'd expect to attempt to solve a mystery. But in the great card game of life, you have to play the hand dealt to us. When a conundrum plops down into your lap, it would be inconsiderate not to at least try your best to unravel it. Besides, I've found that even without great intelligence, skill, dexterity, and social grace, I have been blessed with an uncanny abundance of dumb luck, something you cannot acquire even with a degree from MIT.

And so, fully clad, I set off at one in the morning to meet a total stranger in the ruined shell of Notre Dame church, a house of worship my wife and I loved back in the days before it was closed, stripped of stained glass and other accoutrements, and left to corrode while developers and preservationists bickered over its fate. I had no idea how I'd get through the six-foot chain-link fence, much less open the sure-to-be-locked doors. As a kid, I admired classmates who could leap a fence with only one hand on its railing, but I had no illusions about what would occur if I attempted to replicate the feat myself. Having only recently donned a decent set of pants, I was in no hurry to see them ripped at the crotch after I fell ignominiously from the chain-link pinnacle. No, I would have to find a gap in the fence or go home empty-handed. I don't need an agent to say on my behalf, "He doesn't do his own stunts." I don't do stunts, period.

If I found myself confined to a wheelchair like Raymond Burr in *Ironsides*[1], recovering from a broken leg like Jimmy Stewart in *Rear Window*[2], enormously obese like Nero Wolfe, or an octogenarian like Miss Marple, I could be excused for letting a six-foot fence deter me. However, as a fifty-nine-year-old long-distance runner, I have no excuse to offer. Six feet might as well be six hundred feet. I get afraid of heights standing on the toilet in my bathroom to change a light bulb, although that's a bad comparison. Sometimes, the seat wiggles precariously when you stand on it. I can't tell you how many times I've almost hit my head on the sink while falling at a remarkable velocity from atop the toilet. Frankly, I think Einstein underestimated the rate of acceleration due to gravity and Galileo didn't get it when he suggested that heavier items don't fall faster than objects of the same mass with different weight.

As luck would have it, though (see, I told you I was lucky), an open gate admitted me with ease just as the main doors to the church did. Unfortunately, once those doors swung shut, I couldn't see a darned thing—ironic, because I have had excellent eyesight since birth. Despite my lifelong desire for glasses, my right eye registered twenty/twenty and my left comprised a virtual telescope until I reached the age of forty-nine when my night vision moved on without a forwarding address. After over-shooting more than a few exits and terrifying my children by creating my own nocturnal lanes on the highway, nature fulfilled my desire for corrective lenses. Those optical miracles have kept me literate and mobile, but they certainly do not qualify as night vision goggles. In fact, I think they make the dark seem even darker, if that's possible.

Darkness never was my favorite thing. My sister Christine used to hide in my dark bedroom when I was a child and scare me. When I was in high school, I saw a horror movie on television about a lady dragged down into an abyss hidden in her cellar by creatures that lurk in the dark. Just as prudence keeps me from leaping over fences, it directs me to skedaddle forthwith from pitch-dark places. You may think that, as a one-time Boy Scout, I'd be prepared for ocular challenge by bringing a flashlight, but remember: I'm the guy who set out with no pants. Also, I hold the record for the least promoted scout in history, having spent four years as a Tenderfoot, although I won election as leader of the Beaver Patrol, a unit with a much-coveted patch.

I used to have a terrific mag light that would have worked perfectly for this situation, but a Transportation Safety Authority agent took it from me at Logan Airport because he said it could be used as a weapon. A strange decision, particularly since the airline bumped me to first class, where the flight attendant gave me champagne in a glass flute and dinner cutlery including a steel steak knife. Go figure. And last, no matter how dramatically flashlights illuminate scenes in movies, they serve in reality as pretty pathetic tools for actually dispelling the dark. Consequently, I did not plan to wait around to learn whether or not Notre Dame had a basement with an abyss.

But before I could make my escape, a man—standing not six feet away from me—struck a match, lit a cigarette, activated an LED lantern, and said, "Scott Schaeffer-Duffy, I presume."

Startled but not unhinged, I remonstrated him, "You can't smoke in church."

"It's not a church anymore," he replied. "It's a meeting place for you and I."

"Me," I said.

"What?" he asked.

"It may not still be an official church, but it definitely is a meeting place for you and *me*."

Confused, but determined, he continued, "Given your reputation, I assume you are the person that I need to meet."

"*Whom*," I countered. "*Whom* you need to meet."

"Bloody hell. I'll never get farther along if you keep interrupting me."

Nonplussed, I felt compelled to say, "Further along. 'Farther' implies a measurable distance."

"Son of a picayune porcupine!" he blurted. "Cut the shit! Are you really the activist who went to war zones and jail?"

"Language," I offered. Before he could smack me, I added, "As unbelievable as it is to you and to me, I am he."

"While I have my doubts, it's too late in more ways than one for me to find someone else I can trust. You'll have to do, but, I swear to God, if you correct my grammar once more, I'll hit you so hard you'll explode."

"Is that even possible?" I wondered to myself as he went on.

"I saw a dead guy on Water Street."

"When did you see the body?" I asked.

"I didn't say nothing about a body," he answered.

It took all my willpower and desire for self-preservation to ignore the double negative and admit, "I don't understand."

He merely repeated, "The guy was dead. I know he was. I killed him myself."

"You've lost me," I offered.

"We got in a fight Saturday night outside The Dive Bar. He pulled out a gun, but I moved faster with my knife and stabbed him. He fell forward and drove the knife deeper into his chest. I've been around the horn. I know when a guy is dead, and that's what he was."

The Dive Bar

"I read the *Telegram & Gazette* every day," I countered, "but I didn't see any mention of a stabbing death."

"Neither did I," he replied. "That was the first weird thing, but it meant nothing compared to seeing him come out of the Broadway yesterday morning. Not only was the creep alive. He caught my eye and grinned at me before jumping into a Red Cab."

Unimpressed, I offered, "Apparently, you misjudged his condition."

He grabbed my wrist and said emphatically, "I'm telling you, he was dead! No one walks away from a wound like he had. It's just not possible."

I eased his hand away and said, "Okay, if that's the case, then the man you saw at the diner couldn't have been the same one you stabbed. Maybe he has a twin. Maybe it's just someone with a remarkable resemblance to your victim."

"No," he insisted. "The guy had a red birthmark on his left hand. I saw it clearly when he went for his gun and saw it again when he reached for the cab door. It was almost like he wanted me to see it. The smile on his face gave me the willies."

"Well," I said, "if he reached for a gun and you stabbed him, you might claim self defense in court. The fact that his fall made the wound more serious was purely accidental."

"You're not listening to me," he said. "I'm not worried about the cops or court. I heard you wrote a book with a chapter about supernatural evil, something you walked away from unharmed. I'm a pretty tough guy, not afraid of anyone, but that doesn't mean I'm not afraid of any*thing*. What I saw on Water Street was unnatural. I'm not going to stick around to see it again but wanted to tell someone who might be able to do something about it."

"Whoa!" I blurted. "You've got the wrong man. You can't believe everything you read in the papers. I'm actually quite squeamish. I'm a regular sideshow of phobias. Did you even read my book? There's an entire chapter on hypochondria, for crying out loud. My 'Haunted Hallway' chapter is more of a case of running faster from evil than defeating it. Trust me. I'm not your guy."

"Maybe not," he said, "but it's too late to tell anyone else. I'm outta here. You'll recognize him by the mark on his hand." And without another word, he doused the lantern and left me at the mercy of the darkness.

Tuesday, April 17

I have a remarkably low tolerance for pain. As a kid, I cried during haircuts, so you can well imagine my antipathy to dentistry. I will do just about anything to avoid having to hear the odious words, "Open wide." While no one enjoys getting a root canal, my hysteria begins when a dentist starts invading my mouth with a pick, probing for exposed nerves, and doing everything possible to choke me with blood spurting out of my beleaguered gums. I identify completely with Dustin Hoffman in *Marathon Man*[3]. The sound of a dentist's drill doubles my blood pressure. A normal person gets a sore tooth and goes promptly to his or her dentist to ensure that a tiny cavity never becomes a gaping hole. A normal person is prudent and probably saves himself or herself pain in the long run. Despite coaching cross country and running more than two thousand miles a year, I am all about the short run when it comes to pain. I ignore a toothache and bargain with God for a miraculous healing. But the dull pain nags for attention. It reminds me that I have to do what I do not want to do. Ultimately, I cannot ignore it.

The macabre tale I heard at Notre Dame proved worse than a toothache. I resolved to put the implausible details out of my mind. I planned to avoid the area of the Broadway Diner and The Dive Bar. Although the odds of my running into a single ghoul in a city of 181,004 people ranked extremely low, I vowed to take no chances and averted my eyes whenever I thought I might end up seeing anyone's left hand. If I never saw the birthmark, I'd never have to investigate anything. You'd be surprised how hard it was to pull that off. So the prospect of seeing a dead man walking weighed on me, filled me with apprehension, and obliterated my inner calm. While I desperately tried to deny it, I knew deep down that confrontation with that zombie was inevitable.

Zombie! Now there's a concept I have come to fear in particular. I've seen dozens of zombie movies and TV shows. They do not end well. Even Max Brook's book *World War Z*[4] leaves the door open for a recurrent zombie apocalypse. His *Zombie Survival Guide*[5] purports to offer "complete protection from the living dead," but I don't buy it. Millions of things can go wrong when you try to cope with zombies.

My youngest son, Aiden, relishes a live-action, role-playing, post-apocalyptic game called *Dystopia Rising* with a central focus on zombies and the undead. I should probably ask Aiden how to manage with zombies. I'm sure he knows from experience that the living dead have graduated from shuffling marionettes anyone could outrun to manic creatures that run faster than Usain Bolt. Some experts now believe you can be zombified by as little as a drop of blood or saliva. How the heck can you avoid getting blood or saliva in eyes, mouth, or a cut when you are dispatching hordes of zombies? From what I've seen and read, zombie splatter verges on the insane.

I know what I'm talking about. In my thirty-two years of sheltering the homeless as a member of the Catholic Worker movement, I've had some experience with blood. Especially back in the early days of the AIDs epidemic, people commonly treated blood like radioactive material. We had a prescribed list of precautions to take if someone with the virus got a cut or threw up. For some peculiar reason, when I had to clean up either fluid from the bathroom or kitchen floor, I did so without fear. Why a real disease invokes less terror in me than fictional maladies remains a mystery, not unlike my composure under gunfire in war zones. As a peace activist, I've stared down armed and angry soldiers without breaking a sweat, but I scream uncontrollably when I get a paper cut. A doctor once tried to calm me down by saying, "There, there now. You only need two stitches."

"*Two??*" I replied in escalating agitation. "I thought I only needed one!"

To make matters worse, the weather has started to improve. What does that have to do with anything? Even in this era of global warming, most Worcesterites don gloves or mittens in the winter, but spring amounts to a crap shoot: some days you need 'em, and some days you don't. If it were December, the odds of my seeing someone's hands would be much lower than on April 18. The typical ten-day forecast varies from snow showers to sixty-degree sunshine. If it gets that hot, I might not see only the monster's hand but its arms and legs, too. Jiminy Cricket! Nothing seems to go my way.

Not too long ago, I reviewed my friend Chris Douçot's fine book *No Innocent Bystanders: Becoming an Ally in the Struggle for Justice*[6]. He makes a convincing case that the conceit of those who try to overcome evil without allies dooms them to failure. Gandhi and MLK worked shoulder to shoulder with many others. Even an anti-social character like Sherlock Holmes found solace in sleuthing alongside Dr. Watson. Maybe I need to look for an ally.

Then again, in *Rosemary's Baby*[7] and *The Invasion of the Body Snatchers*[8], the trusted friend turns out to be one of *them* in the end. Add to that the distinct possibility that most people would consider my concern a sure sign of mental instability.

Maybe I'm doomed to fly solo. Still, if sheltering the homeless has taught me anything, you absolutely cannot take people at their word. One woman told me she and Elvis Presley had been close friends. A guy explained he had to kill rats the size of dogs in his basement. Many dozens have insisted on their sobriety when all evidence suggested the contrary. A lifelong New Englander adopted an English accent and started saying he was born in Liverpool before he toured the world as the lead guitarist in a rock band. One insisted aliens had held him captive for seven years. Just about everyone exaggerates how quickly they expect to be back on their feet.

Experience has also taught me not to dismiss anyone's story out of hand. At the Catholic Worker in Washington, DC, a guy named Billy insisted that he was moving to Tahiti and months later sent us a postcard from the South Pacific to prove it. In Worcester, a gay union organizer told us that his close friend, conservative columnist William F. Buckley Jr., would send us a donation and, sure enough, Buckley sent us five hundred dollars. A young man claimed to have written a hit song for the band U2, a tale verified by a hand-written note from U2's lead man, Bono himself, with a bunch of VIP passes to a sold-out concert. We had an intern whose grandfather publishes *The New Yorker* and a guest whose uncle wrote *Fahrenheit 451*[9]. We even hosted someone who directed SAVAK, the secret police of the Shah of Iran. Sometimes preposterous stories represent actual fact. That circumstance tempers my skepticism without making me a Pollyanna and provides a formula for leaving the door open a crack to stories told in the dark by strange strangers.

Thankfully, I'm kept so busy at Saints Francis and Thérèse Catholic Worker that I'm easily distracted. Sheltering homeless people, working for peace and justice, writing, running, parenting, grandparenting, and husbanding pack my days.

After returning from Notre Dame this morning, I grabbed a few hours' sleep, got up, and joined the 5 at 5 group of running maniacs who gather each Tuesday and Thursday at five A.M. to run five miles. Then I did the house laundry and grocery shopping, cleaned the upstairs kitchen and bathroom, answered mail, and went to our weekly peace vigil in Lincoln Square.

The vigil began in 1991 during the lead-up to the first Gulf War. We figured it wouldn't last too long, but the United States has been at war ever since. On cold winter Tuesdays, I've often wanted to hold a sign that says, "End the Wars • Let the Protesters Go Home." In 1991, we had as many as five hundred people weekly. Today, six of us vigiled. On some particularly crappy days, I've stood there by myself but must confess that, on those occasions, I've often endured only a metric hour[10]. Besides me today, we had

> Barbara and Arthur Roberts; she was an engineer in the nuclear weapons industry, and he was a career military officer
>
> Dave Williams, a Lebanese-American poet, editor of our community newspaper *The Catholic Radical*, volunteer at our bakery, and dear friend
>
> Dave Maciewski, a former longtime member of Saints Francis and Thérèse house; he once saved a man's life from an oncoming train
>
> John, a marvelous young man whose last name escapes me

When I returned to the house, my wife, Claire, rang the dinner bell, a brass souvenir from a close encounter she and our infant son, Aiden, had with a bull in the foothills of the Himalayas back in 1995.

Aiden, who graduated from college with a degree in studio art and works in a stained-glass business, sat on my right and Claire, on my left. As per her custom, my wife encouraged everyone to talk. She hates it when folks scarf down their meals in silence like prison inmates. As a very creative person with a nose ring, ever-changing hairdo, and a quote from H. P. Lovecraft tattooed on his arm (not my idea: trust me), Aiden contributes to the conversation while paying closer attention to what others say more often than I do.

When Claire asked a new guest named John, "Are you Italian?" Aiden raised an eyebrow and smiled. I had no idea why.

After dinner, he chuckled, "That question was a no brainer."

"What do you mean?" I asked.

"Didn't you notice his hand?" he asked in return.

With furrowed brow and the odious sound of a dental drill revving up in the back of my mind, I replied, "No."

"He has a big-ass tattoo," Aiden continued, "of a shamrock with a swastika in the middle of it."

Torn between relief that it wasn't a red birthmark and consternation over how Saint Patrick's metaphor for the Holy Trinity could be conflated with Nazism, I agreed that the tattoo provided pretty conclusive proof that John was not Italian.

Washing dishes and setting up a platter of cheese and crackers for a singalong we hosted at seven subsumed even the reminder of unusual markings on a hand. Dan Burke, a fantastic pianist and singer, led us in tunes as diverse as *Finnegan's Wake*, *Let It Be*, *The Piano Man*, and *Sweet Caroline*. I printed books with the lyrics and photos of the artists. Members of the funk band Sly and the Family Stone look particularly wild in huge Afros and bell-bottoms. Our offerings ranged from sixty and seventy-year-old Cole Porter and Bing Crosby songs to the seventies heavy metal hits of Metallica and today's pop rock offerings by Smash Mouth. Stevie Wonder's *A Place in the Sun* is a special favorite.

The gatherings on Mason Street at the Saints Francis and Thérèse Catholic Worker take me back to my childhood. Every Friday night, my entire family—cousins, aunts, and uncles—came together at my grandparents' house for food, drink, and singing. It was really rousing, and I had the impression my clan's practice was not unique.

After the Mason Street sing-a-long concluded, folks disbanded. Claire drove our poet friend, Dave Williams, home. I got a phone call from Cathy, one of our guests, from her room on the second floor. In the age of cell phones, I suppose it shouldn't have surprised me. She said she needed to see Claire, whom I informed after she returned home. Claire went upstairs and came right down to get sanitary napkins and cleaning supplies. She told me she needed to strip the bedding because it had blood on it. While such accidents occur once in a while, it disconcerted me to hear the word "blood" after much dwelling on it.

After soaking the mattress cover and sheets in cold water, Claire gave me instructions on how to wash them at the laundromat come morning. Wouldn't it be a wonderful world if all its problems could be tidied up so easily?

Unfortunately, we don't live in such a world. On my way out the door for an eight-mile run with Karen Pajer, my marathon training partner, our South Indian guest (who overstayed his visa and doesn't like us to use his name in print) informed Claire and me that an ambulance took Cathy to the hospital at one in the morning because she was vomiting and bleeding.

By the time I finished my run, Saint Claire had cleaned the bedroom, kitchen, and bathroom. Claire sent me again to the laundromat. During my absence, Cathy called from the hospital to say she had a bad reaction to an abortion pill. She lost a lot of blood, she said, but would be okay. I couldn't help reflecting on the oppression of the vulnerable. While it takes a woman and a man to conceive a child, all too often only the woman and child bear the consequences. Women, children, gays, lesbians, immigrants, refugees, religious and ethnic minorities, people of color, the homeless, the unborn, the disabled, and the elderly suffer so much at the hands of others.

Coincidentally, seven of our friends—five of them members of the Catholic Worker movement—entered the US submarine base in King's Bay, Georgia, this week on the fiftieth anniversary of the death of Martin Luther King Jr. Among other things, they carried baby bottles filled with their blood to denounce nuclear weapons and call for disarmament. Christians believe Jesus's blood simultaneously represents his suffering on the cross and humanity's redemption from sin. Especially in a country like ours where lethal consequences of war are so distant, some religious activists pour their blood at military installations as a stark reminder of war's human cost and as an appeal for conversion to peace.

For my part, the convergence of so many perplexing events in so short a time filled me with apprehension. Not only did I become convinced that, inevitably, I would see the undead man, but I also grew sure that blood would figure prominently in the encounter. Synchronicity is one of my least favorite things. Though I find it a harmless enough phenomenon when it entails, say, giraffes, tulips, and kites, I find it less appealing when it evokes repeat appearances of tarantulas, jellyfish, and hornets—or *blood*.

Thursday, April 19

Despite my grim prognostication, I survived two days without seeing Mr. Red Hand, a moniker not to be confused with the racist jab about catching someone red-handed. Admittedly, I did spend a lot of my public time with downcast eyes, a technique that caused me to bump into several strangers—all with spotless hands, thanks be to God—in the grocery store.

The eyes-down approach did enrich me, though. You see, last February, after Claire worried that our lives as Catholic Worker volunteers would leave us nothing for retirement, I began collecting change in a large ceramic mug labeled "World's Greatest Author" (my daughter Grace gave it to me. I've always thought daughters had the keenest insight). My rule of thumb is that only funds found on the ground qualify as fair game. Change from normal transactions goes into a large plastic cup representing a clown with a flip-top hair piece. My finders-keepers approach seems unlikely to secure us a bungalow in West Palm Beach. Still, I am very happy to say, it rewarded us a quarter yesterday and three pennies this morning, bringing our total up to $77.55. At that rate, we could have more than four hundred dollars by the time I turn sixty-five. Of course, such a lofty figure depends on people continuing to carry and drop cash. Increased purchases by check, debit card, or credit card could reduce retirement for Claire and me to one night at the Shifty Hotel.

Feel free to add cashless society to my list of phobias.

I typically spend much of my Thursdays in a change-on-the-ground desert also known as the Phelan Center behind Blessed Sacrament Church. We rent an industrial kitchen there to make baked goods for our cottage industry that Claire named The Bread-Not-Bombs Bakery. We bake carrot raisin bran muffins, cinnamon swirls, and loaves of Italian, Irish soda, oatmeal raisin, honey wheat, and buttermilk white bread that we take to different Catholic churches where we offer them before and after Mass for whatever a person wants to give us. Most weeks, the average donation far exceeds anything we'd dare to charge. The cash income covers about half our expenses, and appearing in so many parishes connects us to lots of people. It's a win-win, even if it does make our weekends hectic.

Actual baking starts very early Friday morning and runs through Saturday afternoon. On Thursdays, I shop for supplies and go to the kitchen to deliver them, grease bread pans, and make dry mixes. A beat-up radio keeps me company while I work. I virtually never see anyone there save Jeff, the affable parish custodian, whose pristine hands reveal him as a self-respecting janitor.

You would think such harmless activity would calm my nerves, but it did not. You see, the kitchen, a windowless room with no back door, is located just off a gymnasium. Should a zombie or, heaven forbid, a bunch of zombies invade the gym, I'd be trapped like a hot dog vendor at a PETA Rally. The sturdy doors would hold back an average horde, but I'd eventually starve to death. As someone who once fasted outside the United Nations for twenty-six days, I can assure you that would not be fun.

To add to my growing alarm, Thursday's bakery set-up is only the first stage of our bread-baking sequence. As early as three in the morning on Friday, I have to begin the actual baking and, at that grim hour, even Jeff is not around. I am by myself—solitary, all alone in the dead of night.

By the way, why is it called "the dead of night"? We don't have a corollary "dead of day." While I think of it, how come something can "drive me crazy," but it can't "drive me nervous"? Language is a funny thing. I think I'm the only person who refers to the Ides of April, for example.

I mix, knead, and bake bread at least 120 minutes before vampire rush hour. If the power went out, as it does over and over nowadays in Puerto Rico (thanks a lot, Trump), I'd be plunged into, you guessed it, pitch darkness. I'd be miles into the abyss before Claire even got up for her morning meditation. Since they'd never find my body, I'd be relegated to a measly memorial service instead of a proper funeral. Maybe I'd eventually reappear like Rip Van Winkle, but I sincerely doubt it. Scaling the wall of an abyss requires special skills that a person who cannot surmount a chain-link fence does not possess.

You might think the radio would soothe my savage breast, but it too is a two-edged sword. I'm the first to admit that the BBC's *Hard Talk*, NPR's *Story Corps*, and WBUR's *Curiosity Desk* take my mind off my own petty worries. Unfortunately, there are plenty of stories about famine, war, racism, sexism, and environmental catastrophe to pump up my anxiety. And then there's the miniscule possibility of a *Twilight Zone* moment. Most people would not even consider such poop-yourself-in-the-pants events, but most people haven't spent a summer in an apartment with a gateway to Hell (for details, buy my first book *Nothing Is Impossible: Stories from the Life of a Catholic Worker*[11], available for just $24.95 if you act now).

In a world where someone like Scott Pruitt could lead the Environmental Protection Agency, what's to prevent a radio from broadcasting Beelzebub's voice? "Can't happen," you say, but remember. I just had a meeting with a dude who says he saw a dead man catch a taxi. Most of us would say that can't happen, either. From what I witnessed in Bosnia during the 1992-1995 civil war, I'd be hesitant to rule anything out. One day, I waded through worthless piles of currency in a blown-up Yugoslavian bank and then watched a boy undergo an operation without anesthesia. Someone or something pushes back the parameters of reality just about every day.

I'll tell you one thing. I intend to turn the radio on while I bake, but I also intend to keep one eye on it. If it goes off the rails, I'll have its supernatural behind in the dumpster before you can say "Marconi."

And, sorry to say, a tidy solution to one problem often raises another. My dumpster tactic would put me outside the building, in the dark. As my Swedish grandmother often exclaimed, "Herregud in himel![12]" I could still be supernaturally screwed. What if I forgot the key inside the building? The grim possibilities are endless.

Years earlier, when we baked our bread in the convent attached to Saint Peter Marian High School, I locked myself outside at 4 A.M. with an oven full of baking bread. Clad in short sleeves, an apron, and pants (back in the day when I always remembered to put them on), I stood in the snow and panicked. It was a holiday weekend. If I couldn't get into the building before forty-five minutes elapsed, the bread would burn. A longer delay would cause it to catch fire, set off the fire alarm, and lose us this baking venue for all time. If I couldn't get inside, I could imagine no good outcomes.

I circumnavigated the huge building and looked without success for an open door. I checked also for an open window and, to my delight, found one. With some trepidation, I climbed inside and found my way through a classroom to the hall and eventually to the inside entrance to the convent, which proved to be locked as well. I looked up at the ceiling and wondered if I could fit inside a heating vent. Since the ceilings were more than ten feet high, that was out of the question. I went back outside and finally discovered a second-floor window ajar in the convent wing. I drove my car as close to the side of the building as possible, got up on its roof, and managed to get back inside the building. I arrived in the kitchen just as the timer went off to tell me the bread was ready.

Why, this morning I was so preoccupied that I put cinnamon in the dry mix for Irish soda bread. We've had other catastrophes like putting baking soda instead of baking powder in our muffins, finding our kitchen overrun by ants, spilling a five-gallon bucket of molasses, and getting an electric shock from an ill-considered attempt to raise our doughs more quickly using an electric wok filled with water to create steam. As a person who drowned in a kitchen sink may be wont to complain in the afterlife, "You're not safe anywhere."

Friday, April 20

My alarm went off this morning at 2:50 A.M. With
the weary muscles of a fifty-nine-year-old marathon-
er-in-training, I sprang out of bed and paid special attention
toward donning essential clothing. Once the cobwebs parted
in my brain, I climbed into our 2009 Prius, put in the insanely
over-priced so-called key, and heard lovely guitar music
emanating from the CD player. Claire went to her weekly
meditation meeting last night and must have left the CD
player on.

Our children compiled dozens of CDs so they could
control the music during long rides to relatives in Washington, DC, and northern New Hampshire. Now and then,
they threw in a bone for Claire and me. What I heard was
one such song. It's by Death Cab for Cutie.

Where are all the normal band names like Twisted Sister,
The B52s, and the Dead Kennedys? I once saw a marquee in
Worcester that read: "Tonight only! Rash of Stabbings & The
Boogers".

I wondered if Claire had left the lovely song cued up
for me in sympathy for my having to rise so early. I eagerly
awaited the soothing vocals:

> Love of mine, some day you will die,
> but I'll be close behind.
> I'll follow you into the dark.
> No blinding light or tunnels to gates of white,
> just our hands clasped so tight,
> waiting for the hint of a spark.
> If Heaven and Hell decide
> that they both are satisfied, and

illuminate the No's on their vacancy signs.
If there's no one beside you,
when your soul embarks,
then I'll follow you into the dark.

It's a really sweet song, but it never got very far. Less than five measures in, the CD began making the garbled sound that signifies it's never going to play that song again. Claire, a person of great faith, always insists that if we take the CD out and gently wipe it, the disc revives, but it never works. The highly touted replacement for cassettes and vinyl with its promise of better sound and greater durability, the CD more often than not turns out as fragile as toilet paper. Sometimes you can skip over a defective song, which I tried to do, but no sound emitted from the speakers, so I skipped ahead again. Still nothing. And again, on and on, until I came 'round to the same few notes that teased me with their false promise of "I'll Follow You into the Dark."

Unfortunately, the title reminded me where I was going. Park Avenue, like many American streets, was still ten times more brightly lit at 3 a.m. than just about any Third World city I've ever visited, but Pleasant Street belied its name by sporting fewer lights. The parking lot behind Blessed Sacrament Church, nestled at the foot of the Newton Hill woods, is even dimmer. I did not look forward to entering the pitch dark Phelan Center all by myself, even though I intended to lock the door behind me once I got inside. After all, a villain could already be inside, and I don't have Audrey Hepburn's advantage in *Wait Until Dark*[13]. I felt like the character in *Galaxy Quest*[14] who begs to go on a mission to an unknown planet's surface because he fears he'll be killed if he were left

The Phelan Center

behind—only to realize that once on the planet he fears being killed there as well.

My brother Chipper likes to say, "Everything is already written in the Book." Lock the door, leave it unlocked, turn left, turn right—no matter. If you are doomed, that's all there is to it.

With such morose thoughts percolating in my brain even as I passed innocuous places like the gas station with one-dollar coffee, no matter what size, and attendants who speak Arabic, I thought of the orchestral score used in the opening scene of Stanley Kubrick's *The Shining*[15]. Although what appears on screen is harmless footage of a car driving up a beautiful mountain road on a sunny day, the music conveys a terrifying sense of foreboding. If our lives had a sound track and I heard that music playing, I'd change my plans instantly.

It's true that I would not find employment as the off-season caretaker of the haunted Overlook Hotel like Jack Nicholson in *The Shining*, but—hoping no one lurked inside—I remained resolved to enter a dark edifice.

As I turned into the parking lot, however, it surprised me to see the windows of the second-floor gymnasium ablaze with light. Probably the previous night's basketball players forgot to turn out the lights. Father Richard Trainor, the eager pastor of Blessed Sacrament, wants the building used by as many groups as possible. The gym not only hosts basketball, but baseball, soccer, and volleyball teams. It also transforms into a nice space for receptions, dances, and meetings. Entirely comprised of refugees from Burma, the volleyball team is especially talented.

Seeing the light should have eased my disquiet, but, since I'm a contrary person, it did not. After all, Jack Nicholson saw the ballroom lights on and discovered a crowd of dancing revelers who turned into cadavers before his eyes.

You see, most of us make the mistake of assuming that only certain people, things, and places, like cemeteries, are scary. In actual fact, the most ordinary and even non-threatening things can purvey terror. For example, several horror movie franchises base themselves on murderous dolls. In *Sorry, Wrong Number*[16], we learn to fear telephones. In *Invasion*[17], we find that sleep is fatal. In *The Stuff*[8], we're doomed if we eat yogurt. In *The Ring*[19], we die if we watch a certain video. In *It's Alive*[20], we have to avoid a mass murdering infant. In *Gremlins*[21], we can't spill water on cute pets. In *They Live*[22], special sunglasses reveal monsters. In *The Birds*[23], seagulls peck our eyes out. In *High Anxiety*[24], we're not safe from pigeons.

So, I anticipated that those lights on in the gym, something I had never seen on a Friday morning before, could be a very bad omen.

Or, as I learned after I went inside, it was just an empty gym with its lights on.

We have to be careful not to work ourselves up over nothing.

In *Duck Soup*[25], Groucho Marx plays Rufus T. Firefly, the leader of Freedonia, a nation that has just declared war against its neighbor Sylvania because its ambassador called Marx's character an upstart. After the ambassador offers to apologize, Groucho agrees to a reconciliatory meeting, but while waiting he says,

> I'd be unworthy of the high trust that's been placed in me if I didn't do everything within my power to keep our beloved Freedonia at peace with the world.
>
> I'd be only too happy to meet Ambassador Trentino and offer him the right hand of good fellowship on behalf of my country. I feel sure he would accept my gesture in the spirit I would offer it.
>
> But suppose he doesn't. A fine thing that'll be. I hold out my hand and he refuses to accept it. That'll add a lot to my prestige, won't it? Me, the head of a country, snubbed by a foreign ambassador. Who does he think he is that he can come here and make a sap out of me in front of all my people?
>
> Think of it—I hold out my hand and that hyena refuses to accept it. Why, the cheap, four-flushing swine! He'll never get away with it, I tell you. He'll never get away with it!

When the unsuspecting ambassador arrives, Groucho shouts, "So, you refuse to shake hands with me, eh?" and slaps him.

Despite Groucho's chutzpah, the *Shining*'s frightful overture keeps me on my toes like the sound of the dentist drill in the back of my mind.

Saturday, April 21

The last twenty-four hours have been a roller coaster ride, something I feared as a child and still loathe.

It began innocently on Friday when, after I finished wrapping the bread, I drove to Saint Joseph's Abbey in nearby Spencer where Trappist monks chant psalms six times a day and support themselves making preserves and brewing beer. As far back as the 1940s, Dorothy Day, the cofounder of the Catholic Worker, had a close relationship with that contemplative religious order. She and the monk Thomas Merton of the Abbey of Gethsemane in Kentucky stood as key religious opponents of the Vietnam War. Ten years before the Saints Francis and Thérèse Catholic Worker opened, the Mustard Seed Catholic Worker five blocks away from our house had a close relationship with Saint Joseph's Abbey. We at Saints Francis and Thérèse enjoy a similar bond.

Each Friday morning, I drive past the little gift shop at the entrance to the Trappists' property, up the wooded hill, and into the monastic enclosure where visitors find vast hay fields, tree-lined lanes, and an energy center, car port, tailor shop, laundry, bakery, and brewery. A separate road leads past retreat houses and entrances to the Romanesque-style chapel. Until the early 1970s, the monks took vows of stability and silence. In those days, they communicated with each other in writing or by sign language. With few exceptions, they spoke out loud only during prayer. Nowadays, monks can talk freely throughout much of each day.

On that Friday, after navigating my way past a huge flock of wild turkeys, I pulled up to the back door of the monastery's kitchen where Brother Jude Corden greeted me warmly.

He put together three or four boxes overflowing with food that we use at Saint Francis and Thérèse house and also share with our neighbors. Because of the Trappists, we seldom have to buy coffee, pasta, hot chocolate, honey, olive oil, English muffins, jelly, or jam. One week, he gave us a huge wheel of Gouda cheese. In the summer, the monks share vegetables from their garden. Beyond their material largess, the Trappists also keep us and our work in their prayers, something we appreciate very much.

Claire and I sometimes brought our children to Saint Joseph's for Mass. Our oldest son Justin had such fond memories of the monastery that he chose it as the place to propose to his wife, Patricia Kirkpatrick.

After returning from the monastery to Worcester, distributing the food, picking up our guests' laundry, grocery shopping, and wrapping the bread, I helped watch our cherubic two-year-old grandson, Theo. With a tip of my hat to Theodore Cleaver from 1950s television, I call him the Beaver. Theo's mother, our daughter Grace, works for the Regional Environmental Council, Inc. What with her mother-in-law, friends, Claire, and me, Theo is well looked after while Grace works. In the afternoon, Claire took him to the Ecotarium, Worcester's impressive science museum packed with kids during school vacation week. He delighted in seeing playful otters and the other children, too, although his first ride on the train around the grounds left him a bit shell-shocked.

"What the heck is this thing?" he seemed to wonder.

At 4:30, Theo's cousins May and Frances joined him at our house. Claire calls four-year-old May "The Madame," and we all call her two-year-old sister "Shifty." Frances earned her nickname by quietly seeking out phones, remote controls, and calculators, then hiding them. If caught in the act, she grins widely but does not desist. During a visit to Washington, DC, her mother, Patricia, discovered that Shifty had taken a hotel phone across town. All three grandchildren have mastered the cell phone, something I have not. On Friday, Claire's cell rang, and she laughed because Theo had called her from his Uncle Justin's phone.

Our children and grandchildren come over on Fridays because, more than twenty years ago, we began a tradition of holding Family Night at the start of each weekend. We eat with our guests every night of the week except Friday. Claire cooked the meal for the guests and served them upstairs before joining and serving us downstairs. We use Family Night to check in with family members about their week and, after dinner, to do some kind of activity together. We've played games or gone to the movies, hiking, biking, or swimming. We've made costumes or doughnuts. We've roasted marshmallows, dipped candles, carved pumpkins, and more. It has surprised Claire and me how faithful our children have remained to the practice through all the years.

By the time I laid myself down to sleep, I had not a smidgen of anxiety in my mind. My optimism continued on Saturday morning when I went into the bakery at 5:30 A.M. to mix two large buckets of dough for cinnamon swirls. I placed the doughs to rise on top of the convection oven and returned home, where Claire prepared to take over at our bakery. I can make rudimentary swirls, but she's the master of the craft. Mine come out as big as hub caps, while she creates the perfect size. Our customers love her swirls. Mine, not so much.

Claire kneads and rolls out dough. She covers it with butter, brown sugar, and cinnamon paste, sprinkles it with raisins, rolls it up, cuts it into single servings, and lets them rise. Then she bakes, wraps, and labels. During her bakery stint, I don my running gear and go to Worcester State University for a weekly 5K road race hosted by our running club, The Central Mass Striders. At WSU, I meet my marathon pal Karen for a two-mile warm-up which she insists should be no faster than nine minutes per mile. As usual, we finish at 8:43 per mile. She gripes and swears that she will not run the race faster than 8:30 pace. Since we are training together for the May 6 Providence Marathon where we both hope to get fast enough times to qualify for the 2019 Boston Marathon, Karen found an online plan that promises to deliver that goal.

"The 5K is just a training run," she constantly reminds me, while I always push to go faster.

We are working together because she needs to speed up while I need to slow down. Until a year ago, her average 5K pace was eleven minutes and mine was 6:50. She ran her first marathon during the ninety-degree 2011 Boston race. It was a nightmare. Due to extreme heat, the Boston Athletic Association extended the time for runners to complete the race. Karen finished at six hours and twenty minutes. That was also my first marathon. Like Karen, I received a time-waived entry to the Boston Marathon as a reward for volunteering with the Central Mass Striders. During training, I did long runs at a 7:50 pace. I thought I was in top shape on race day, but about two thirds of the way to Boston my quads began torturing me. I limped the remaining eight miles, got passed by a dude dressed as a cheeseburger, and finished over five hours. I was so angry, I ran the Worcester Marathon three weeks later and finished at three hours and thirty-two minutes. That time remained three minutes away from qualifying for the following year in Boston.

So I ran the Bay State Marathon in Lowell to finally achieve my goal at three hours and twenty-seven minutes, just under eight minutes per mile. Unfortunately, I didn't quit while I was ahead. I have completed seven other marathons, all of them disasters where I flew for eighteen miles and then choked my way to the finish. Sometimes, my body fell apart. Sometimes the weather tried to kill me. In Vermont, the wind blew so strong that it nearly ripped the door off the hotel where I stayed the night before the race.

Runners at the 2016 Boston Marathon faced 46-degree rain and a fierce head wind. The following year, I had a 101-degree fever when I ran Boston. I hallucinated my way to a 4-hour, 21-minute finish. I followed it with a stab at Providence but pulled a muscle three days before the race and saw my record time disappear at nineteen miles. I looked so pitiful that, wearing jeans, Claire jumped into the race, to help me finish the last three miles. Due to her encouragement, I managed to cross the finish line in 4 hours and 8 minutes.

And so, Karen and I are well matched. She keeps me from over-training, and I dispel the notion that she cannot go faster. Yesterday's 5K is a good example of the result. I finished with a 7:32 pace and she finished with 7:55, perfect times for our marathon goals.

"I thought you said the last forty-eight hours was a roller coaster," you might remind me.

Thus far, the past forty-eight hours probably reads more like a Tilt-A-Whirl ride. But just when life saunters along happily on a jolly road that seems like it will never end, you have to be extra wary. A piece of space junk could hit you or a loved one.

"Not likely," you say.

Well, Claire and I have a friend whose career as a professional tennis player was sabotaged by an errant skydiver. If she could be clunked on the head by a man with a parachute, anything can happen.

I blame only myself for being lulled into the false hope that I could ignore my meeting at Notre Dame.

On Saturday afternoon, I loaded ten racks of bread, muffins, and swirls into our Prius, a circus-clown-like car with a lot more room inside than you might expect. I set out for Saint Luke's Church in Westborough. Along the way, I stopped at an Indian store in Shrewsbury, the only place where I can buy some of the supplies for my Monday meal of matar paneer.

As the child of a US diplomat, Claire spent five years in India. Through the generosity of our friend, the actor Martin Sheen, Claire and I took our four children there for six wild weeks in 1996. I have since mastered a few recipes. Unfortunately, the Indian proprietors of the market qualify as true anarchists. The posted hours on the door are mere suggestions, distant ideals, or cruel jokes. Yesterday marked my sixth straight visit when I found a note promising a later opening hour. The permanent sign says the store opens on Saturdays at 10 A.M., but the note says 4 P.M., and I wouldn't hold my breath then, either. The mercurial character of the notes remind me of instructions left by the commander in *Catch 22*[26] instructing his subordinates to admit no one to see him unless he had already left.

Saint Luke's is a brick church on the residential end of Westborough's Main Street. Quite affluent, the town once hosted the GTE plant where Barbara Roberts, our friend from the Tuesday peace vigil, helped in the 1980s to engineer the command, control, and communications system for the MX nuclear missile. Many high-paid GTE employees called Saint Luke's their parish. Conversely, the pastor, Father Leo Barry, espoused nonviolence. In the lead-up to the First Gulf War, he put a sign in front of the church that read,

"War in the Persian Gulf would be useless slaughter."

—Pope John Paul II

After a hullabaloo raged in the pews and papers, Father Leo agreed to take the sign down, then replaced it each week with a different papal antiwar message.

The current pastor is Monsignor Mike Foley, a great fan of the Catholic Worker (boy, does he ever sell our baked goods from the pulpit) and genuine Christian. He led the parish to donate ten percent of its weekly income to worthwhile causes, initiate a Spanish liturgy, link itself with a Haitian parish, and champion the environment. Inspired by Pope Francis's 2015 encyclical letter, *Laudato Si*[27], with its concern for the earth, Saint Luke's converted a portion of the parish cemetery into a community garden. At Mass yesterday, which I had forgotten was Earth Day, the congregation prayed,

that we learn about Church teaching on the environment and the impacts of our lifestyles on the poor and vulnerable in our own country and around the world and for the millions of environmental refugees all over the world that have been displaced from their homes because of rising sea levels, droughts, expanding deserts, catastrophic flooding, and other environmental disaster.

As someone who led a Catholic Worker peace team to Darfur, Sudan, I am well aware how global warming destroys habitats, creates conflict, and leads to death by thirst, hunger, and war, but I am not accustomed to hearing such connections made at Mass.

I arrived at Saint Luke's at three. Mass didn't begin until five, so I unloaded the bread onto a big table in the vestibule and went in search of a drink. I had filled a glass bottle with water and a bit of lemon juice but forgot it at home (just another thing I've overlooked of late). Hollis Dunlop, a Providence College student, gave a talk at our house six or seven years ago urging us not to use plastic water bottles. Hers was one of four talks I've heard in my life that actually moved me to action. The others concerned firecrackers, bananas, and a get-rich-quick scheme called The Golden Pyramid. I've never bought or even drunk from a plastic water bottle since Hollis's talk, a feat hard for me to accomplish as a runner.

You'd be amazed how many races terminate at a mountain of plastic water bottles. When Claire and I climbed Crough Patrick in County Mayo, Ireland, what a bummer to see empty bottles all along the trail. A flotilla of water bottles and other junk ruined my one and only swim in the Mediterranean in Haifa. I understand, too, that a mass of plastic debris larger than Texas floats in the Pacific Ocean between San Francisco and Hawaii.

So, you can imagine my quandary when I entered a so-called convenience store to find a drink. When I was a kid, most companies dispensed drinks in glass bottles. In recent years, Snapple held out as one of the few against the plastic invasion, but, due to conservative commentator Rush Limbaugh's sponsorship of Snapple, the product leaves a bad taste in my mouth.

I soon didn't have to worry about that problem, though. Snapple boasts its "New Plastic Bottle!" as if it had accomplished something major. Starbucks often sells a coffee drink in a wide-mouthed glass bottle, but I don't drink coffee. Those who know me agree I'm manic enough without caffeine. An array of eight coolers with six shelves each was filled with plastic from top to bottom. That store alone could add the state of Rhode Island to the floating plastic continent. Finally, I spied Nantucket Nectars, a company begun "by two guys named Tom, a blender and a peach." Despite their failure to use the Oxford comma, I was delighted to see that the company distributes its products in glass.

Exercising another of my idiosyncracies, I slapped down three Eisenhower silver dollars on the counter and enjoyed the "All Natural Ingredients." Later, I filled the empty bottle with water from Saint Luke's bathroom sink and brought the container home with the full intention of congratulating the Toms on their environmental choice. Unfortunately, when I dialed the "Questions or comments?" number, it depressed me to hear, "Thank you for calling Doctor Pepper/Snapple consumer relations."

Is every product owned by a bigger company? Why don't we just use generic labels like in *Repo Man*[28] where white cans that say FOOD or DRINK fill store shelves?

But I digress.

Before I get back to the roller coaster day, though, I have to say that, regardless of the inadvisability of plastic water bottles at road races, the most idiotic thing occurs when sponsors set up water stops along a course with tables full of H_2O in Styrofoam cups. Not only is the stuff eternally toxic, but the friggin' cups explode when you grab them. They remind me of the scene from *Young Frankenstein*[29] when the creature gets nothing to eat or drink from the blind man.

Anyway, at about 4:30, I sat myself in the church vestibule behind a table laden with our baked delights. A fourteen-year-old, red-headed boy and a very tall blond woman, who for some inexplicable reason felt the need to be even taller by wearing high heels, stood on either side of the main doors to greet people as they arrived. Quite a few Mass-goers purchased our baked goods before the service. I gave each of them a copy of our Catholic Worker newsletter, *The Catholic Radical*. Monsignor Foley came over to welcome me. A warm sun streamed in behind me. I remained on the Tilt-A-Whirl.

Until I was six, the Catholic understanding of honoring the sabbath could only be fulfilled by attending a Sunday Mass in Latin. In the middle 1960s, Pope Paul VI borrowed the Jewish convention that a new day begins at sundown rather than sunrise, a technicality that allowed Catholics to fulfill their Sunday obligation on Saturday night. To my surprise, the innovation caught on big time with the elderly. A pastor once told me the Saturday liturgy so teemed with older women that he called it The Blue Hair Mass. But while our Orthodox Jewish sisters and brothers wait for the actual setting of the sun to light the Shabbat candles, Catholics hold Mass anywhere from 4 P.M. on Saturday all the way to 10 P.M. Sunday, a miraculous thirty-hour day.

Don't look at me. I'm not going to rock the boat over that one.

A few minutes before five, the vestibule filled up with eight men and women clad in flowing white hooded robes along with two teens similarly attired. Late arrivals for Mass had to thread their way through that sea of white. Since Monsignor Foley told me he wouldn't be officiating at the Mass, I tried to determine the identity of the celebrant.

"Button, button, who has the button?" I wondered, until I noticed one member of the huge procession holding an ornate lectionary. He had to be a deacon. Two women displayed crosses held around their necks by metal chains. They might be lectors or cantors. The other adults probably were Eucharistic ministers. A teenaged altar boy held a large cross. An altar girl held a candle. By process of elimination, I concluded that the priest had to be the one clad in a robe with an ornate strand of green edging. Confirmation of my supposition came when, as he raised his hand, entrance music began and the entire parade marched up the aisle with him at the rear.

When I sell bread at a church, my policy is to stand in the back throughout Mass. At appointed times, I kneel, but otherwise I stay standing. The reading referred to the Good Shepherd. I found the homily and music reasonably inspiring. By the time everyone recited the Lord's Prayer, I had begun to find a decent spiritual groove—that is until I came to what Catholics euphemistically call "The Kiss of Peace" (there is actually very little kissing in Catholicism) when congregants are encouraged to turn to their neighbors and say "Peace be with you" or anything in that ballpark. A surprising number of grey-haired folks flash the peace sign, which makes me wonder if they had been hippies at Woodstock.

At the appointed moment, I stepped close to the last pew, shook hands with a young man in a plaid shirt, and then repeated the gesture with an older fellow one pew farther up. The second guy was about fifty-five years old, five-foot-ten, weighing about a 190 pounds, in blue jeans and a light tan jacket. When he said "Peace," I happened to look down and noticed a prominent red birthmark on the back of his left hand. The sight so startled me that I almost forgot to return his greeting.

After the guy let go of my hand and turned back toward the altar, my mind raced,

"Was he the belligerent from The Dive Bar?"

He sure didn't look dead to me. His hand didn't feel particularly cadaverish. He had a friendly visage. If I hadn't had that conversation in Notre Dame, I wouldn't have given him a second thought. But as it was, I kept him in sight, waiting to see if he would receive Communion. I'm not sure about zombies or ghouls, but I know for certain, thanks to Bram Stoker, that vampires cannot touch the Communion wafer without burning their flesh. I like to think lots of supernatural villains shrink from consecrated bread, holy water, and all the other cool things in the Catholic arsenal.

He got up from his pew and into the line-up of folks intending to receive Communion.

With three communicants between us, I trailed my suspect up the aisle. Since people processed in two lines, I changed to the faster right lane so I could pull even with him. Glancing furtively, I saw nothing out of the ordinary. I focused so intently on the moment when a Eucharistic minister placed the host on his palm that the priest in front of me cleared his throat as if to say, "May I help you?"

After receiving the Body of Christ, I peeled off to the right of the altar while Mr. Dead-But-Alive went left. He appeared to be unfazed by the sacrament.

Could the Eucharistic minister have been in cahoots with him? Maybe she gave him a dud. That would be pretty slick, but how would she distinguish the unconsecrated wafer from the others?

No. Unless Saint Luke's was distributing nothing but plain old bread, I had to accept that the man in tan had Jesus inside him.

I hoped to garner more information. Unfortunately, so many customers crowded around the bread table I never saw the Catholic cadaver leave.

I would have liked to know if he departed with anyone else, what kind of car he drove, and whether or not he spit out the host into the bushes. Alas, I had nothing more incriminating to consider than the birthmark on his hand, a blemish that might not even be the one that the guy at Notre Dame warned me about.

I stewed over my disappointment until just after seven when the Spanish Mass began. I slipped out to get something to eat. The sun went down as I turned right on Main Street, passed the typical New England white Unitarian and Congregational churches and the Westborough municipal building. Thirty-eight years ago, when I was a senior at Holy Cross, I spent three days with six others in lockup in that building for a Good Friday anti-nuclear protest at GTE. On Easter Sunday, Father Barry convinced the police to allow him to bring us Communion. I'm happy to say, none of my codefendants caught fire when they touched the host.

Darkness fell by the time I arrived at the Subway restaurant, where I enjoyed a terrific sandwich the last time I sold bread at Saint Luke's.

As during my previous visit, no other customers were there.

The clerk, a woman who told me last year that she came from Kerala, India, greeted me with, "A long time since you have been here."

"Wow!" I thought. "She sure does have a good memory."

"Good to see you again, too," I said before placing my order and asking, "Where are all your customers?"

She shrugged and disappeared to the back without a word.

My spider sense began to tingle. How could the place remain in business without a single customer on a Saturday night? How could that woman remember me? More, importantly, how did she remember that I wanted jalapeños on my veggie sub? Was she one of *them*? Was the restaurant even a real Subway? Why had no one passed by as I ate in a storefront booth? Was I in the real Westborough or a clever movie set made up to look like Westborough?

About then, I realized I never should have watched *The Truman Show*[30], *The Matrix*[31], or *Dark City*[32]. Were it not for the truly excellent sandwich, I might have succumbed to paranoia.

When I exited to return to Saint Luke's, I noticed the colonial cemetery on the opposite side of the street. Its thin grey stones tilted slightly backward or forward over the centuries. Surrounding bare trees and unruly grass evoked familiar and friendly horror stories of my youth. I always liked how Scrooge in Charles Dickens's *A Christmas Carol* initially stands up to Marley's ghost and says, "There's more of gravy than grave about you, whatever you are."

My confirmation saint, the apostle Thomas, wouldn't believe Jesus had risen from the dead unless he could put his finger in the nail holes in Christ's hand. Now there's a detective who relies on solid evidence over hearsay. Like Thomas, I had to get a grip, keep rational, and go public only if and when I had an iron-clad case.

Maybe Dustin Hoffman could help me. In *Stranger Than Fiction*[33], Will Ferrell tells Hoffman that he hears Emma Thompson narrating his life, as if it were a novel. Hoffman asks Ferrell a series of questions:

Has anyone left any gifts outside your home? Anything? Gum, money, a large wooden horse?

Do you find yourself inclined to solve murder mysteries in large luxurious houses to which you may or may not have been invited?

On a scale of one to ten, what would you consider the likelihood of your being assassinated?

Are you the king of anything? Anything, king of the lanes at the local bowling alley? King of the trolls? Of a clandestine land found underneath your floor boards?

Was part of you at one time made of something else? Is it possible that your arms were made of stone, wood, lye, corpse parts, or that your birth was made holy by rabbinical elders?

Do you have any magical powers?

After a perplexed Ferrell answers "No" to every question, Hoffman says,

The only way to find out what story you are in is to determine what you are not in. Odd as it may seem, I just ruled out half of Greek literature, seven fairy tales, ten Chinese fables, and determined conclusively that you are not King Hamlet, Scout Finch, Miss Marple, Frankenstein's monster, or a golem.

Since all our lives are stories, Hoffman's method seems sound to me. After all, if I am a character in a romantic comedy, I can rest easy knowing that all will end well. But if I am in a tragedy, things will get worse and worse. A murder mystery entails danger around every corner. A thriller requires body armor while fantasy demands drugs. Sci-fi and horror are mixed bags, most of them appalling downers but some with happy endings.

If I am in a horror or sci-fi story, all bets are off. The apparent innocence of my suspect may be only a red herring, a clever author's device to lull me into complacency only to heighten the effect when the ghastly truth is finally revealed. In fact, if I am a character in poorly written literature, my situation may be hopeless. Bad authors like to drop finales out of thin air, surprises with no basis in the preceding work. I can take such treatment in *Monty Python and the Holy Grail*[34] because those guys were satirical comedians, but in general,

I feel the gross unfairness of inexplicable *deus ex machina*[35] endings.

Nonetheless, despite my preferences, I have to consider everything. So far, I'm afraid the ultimate genre of this book remains to be determined. It could go in many directions, a fact that disconcerts me greatly, as I like to know from a book's jacket what to expect in general. How else can I decide on the safety of reading a particular book alone at night, on an airplane, during a break-up, after a tragic loss, while depressed, or in the months before my semi-annual physical? I don't want to pick up *Tom Sawyer*[36] and see it morph into *The Murders in the Rue Morgue*[37]. Let me tell you, if I don't get a straight answer on the question of genre soon, I'm outta here!

Sunday, April 22

If this morning is any indication, I am in a sports drama/comedy. Karen and I set out together at eight to run fourteen miles. Since I am in slightly better shape and to help distract her, I decided to narrate our run as if we were actually running the Providence Marathon course. Although I have only completed that course twice, I can recall many of its features.

When Karen and I turned left on Mason Street, I said, "And here we are, surrounded by two thousand runners in downtown Providence on Exchange Street with Burnside Park to our right and stately buildings to our left."

As we turned left by the Spanish market and Church's Fried Chicken onto Chandler Street, I said, "And here we go right onto Memorial Boulevard with sky scrapers to our right and the Woonasquatucket River to our left. Brown University is several blocks to our left up a steep hill that, thank God, we do not have to climb."

As we turned left onto Park Ave past State Liquor, I said, "And now, we go left over a beautiful stone bridge and then right onto lovely South Main Street."

You might think I could not keep such a mirage going for fourteen miles, but you'd be very wrong. I have been known to stick with a tried and true gag for decades. Although, I must admit, it felt weird to say, "Finally, we have a nice downhill with trees protecting us from the wind" when we actually ran uphill on Main Street into a headwind.

Our target pace for the day was a nine-minute mile, something we exceeded for the first third of our run, but Karen started to flag after that. Our middle miles clocked dangerously close to 9:45, but thank goodness we rebounded at the end to average 9:10. Maybe my description of the Narraganset Bay off to our right inspired her. Maybe the crescendo of our story will have the two of us breaking the tape in Providence, dancing around with a crown of leaves. After all, as the title of my first book proclaims, *Nothing Is Impossible*.

Monday, April 23

A beautiful spring day, Shakespeare's birthday, our first to reach 60 degrees, I spent doing laundry, shopping, watching my granddaughters, having a weekly house meeting, and preparing an Indian meal. I found three cents to add to our retirement fund (already up to $78.37) and sold two advance copies of my second book, *Murder on Mott Street: a Catholic Worker mystery*[38], a title that plays fair with the reader. I have now sold 1,000 copies of my first book and 17 of the second. At that rate, I will be a best-selling author by 2058. I take solace from the fact that my publisher tells me the average American book, over the last ten years, has sold only 259 copies. When you consider that more than 30,000 books are published annually in the US, that's not surprising. It nevertheless means that most authors lose their shirts and pants instead of getting rich.

The fact that my first book received positive reviews soothes my pride a bit. Early responses to my second book have been, shall we say, less forgiving. Maybe, unlike this opus, it's a niche book, appealing only to very particular readers. Maybe the literary world will discover me posthumously. A lot of good that will do for my ego here and now. But, as my editor, the ever-faithful Marcia Gagliardi, says, "Onward, ever onward!"

Just so. To my delight, our guests loved my meal, something no one can guarantee. At one time, I came up with the idea that diners should rate each meal anonymously on a scale of one to ten and we would reveal the most popular cook at the end of each week. I believed that I, who had worked in restaurants for years, often alongside a chef, could cook as well as Claire and much better than our co-worker Dave Maciewski, but the voters did not concur. They must have misunderstood the scale and thought Number 1 was the highest number. I cannot, even now, contemplate the depressing alternative.

On this glorious day, though, the judgment of our guests was spot-on. They eagerly consumed every morsel served. Five out of six diners had seconds. And enough remained left over for me to take to our Monday night run-and-pot-luck supper in Kelley Square, an intersection of five streets without a single traffic light. It boasts the Hotel Vernon with its prohibition days speakeasy called The Ship Room for reasons obvious to those admitted. Other businesses there include Kelley Square Pizza, C & N Vietnamese Cuisine, two gas stations, the Table Talk Pie Bakery, a Burger King, and a Subway. (Would the same mysterious woman from Westborough be behind its counter?)

Kelley Square also features The Ballot Box Bar, a wonderfully hospitable establishment that welcomes runners to meet, race, and then share food over beer, wine, and other drinks. We typically gather at 6 P.M. for a two-mile warmup followed by a three-mile race at 6:30. Conducted in traffic all year round without any safety monitors, such runs are not for the squeamish. Most participants do not race hard, but some throw caution to the wind. A fellow who ran it in fifteen minutes eight years ago set the record. He may have had an advantage, though, since he ran faster than most cars.

A week before Christmas, our numbers swell when a runner dresses as Santa Claus for a caroling crawl to a fire station, hotel, hospital, several restaurants, and bars along our usual course. Last Christmas had particular drama because our weekly raffle had not drawn a winner for two months and thus had more than $220 in the pot.

Typical of most nights, a vigorous round of trash talk precedes the race. As soon as my friend and rival Vin Garofoli arrived tonight, it began in earnest.

"Hi, Vin," I said. "I didn't expect to see you after what happened Saturday morning at the Worcester State University 5K."

"What are you talking about?" he retorted. "I crushed you."

"Now Vin," I said paternally, "you know I was just doing a training run with Karen but still finished only eight seconds behind you. In fact, I think I gave you a push."

"A push, my ass," Vin answered. "You were at least twenty seconds behind me."

"Memory is the first thing to go with age, Vin. I think you need to check the results."

Carlos Moreira, the nicest guy you could ever meet, whipped out his phone and announced that I had actually run twelve seconds behind Vin.

"See?" I proclaimed. "You said I was *twenty* seconds behind you."

"And you said you were *eight* seconds behind me," Vin insisted.

"*Metric*," I explained patiently.

Everything is different in the metric system. Three miles is almost five kilometers. Six miles is almost ten kilometers, and so on. I love how much faster I get to drive by setting my speedometer on the metric system. I full well expect to live 125 metric years.

The chatter doesn't stop after the race begins. In the first half mile, I said, "Now, Vin, remember what your doctor said about your ticker. If you start feeling a tightness in your chest, don't you worry. As soon as Carlos and I finish the race, we'll come back and give you CPR."

Truth be told, Vin has beaten me many times in a row since I started training with Karen. She insists that we keep to a set pace which does not permit catching him. Even more truthfully, I'm not sure I could catch him most times no matter what. At sixty-two, he's faster than many young men.

But not this night. Not on this Saint Crispin's Day! I refused to hold my manhood cheap and felt fully prepared to strip my sleeves and show my scars. Vin never stood a chance. I passed him at just after mile one. He retook the lead briefly, but I vanquished him for all time at two miles. I can still hear the roar of Mike Morrissey and Carlos as I flew across the finish line.

Meanwhile, Claire and Karen ran a nice, easy, talking-pace run. I don't dare call it a "jog," the ultimate insult. Cautious Karen has convinced herself that I'm going to spoil our marathon by getting injured in the final days.

"I am not afraid of injury," I told her.

"Why not?" she asked.

"Because I'm already injured," I said with authority. "I have pain in my right hip and left ankle that would bring most runners to their knees. But as long as I have injuries on both sides, my balance remains good."

Carlos doubted I could get a speedy hip replacement and recover before the Providence Marathon on May 6, so I am forced to soldier on. People say, "Listen to your body," but I'd never run if I paid attention to that old nag.

I am forgetting myself. Something else went on tonight in Kelley Square. You see, our course passes both the Broadway Diner and The Dive Bar, significant sites in my late-night informant's tale. I must admit, despite my laser-like focus on victory at all costs over Vin, I had some disquiet about passing the spots where he saw Mr. Red Hand. Between the warmup and race, I passed the Broadway and Dive three times each, often enough to consider it a stakeout.

And yet, sorry to disappoint you horror fans, I saw nary a soul, much less one with a red birthmark. That is until I finished the race at Weintraub's Deli. Flush with the thrill of victory, I walked a bit before heading back toward the Ballot Box. In keeping with my custom when running, I stayed in the bike lane facing traffic. A black sedan came toward me up Water Street. The driver had his window down and arm draped on the sill. He slowed as he passed, and I saw, as plain as day, that it was the same man I encountered at Saint Luke's. He passed so close that he could easily have slapped me with his birthmarked hand.

I spun around, hoping to catch his license number. I got only two digits, which I promptly forgot. I did notice that he had a Massachusetts plate on a Ford with a Hillary Clinton bumper sticker. If he indeed drove his own car, I surmised that the zombie was a Roman Catholic Democrat who knew nothing about cars.

Wednesday, April 25

For reasons fleshed out on pages 31-32 of *Nothing Is Impossible*, I feel compelled to give something to every beggar I meet, even if it's nothing more than a sympathetic word. Generally faithful to that compulsion, I must admit that I often act without enthusiasm and not because I am skeptical about a beggar's pitch. I have no interest in trying to vet who is and who isn't one of the deserving poor, and I know from experience how humiliating it is to beg for help. I act without enthusiasm because I don't like others seeing me merely as a conduit of money. I feel bad enough about white privilege without giving poor people the false impression that I'm wealthy, especially when the dude I'm giving to may have more money in his or her pocket than I do. Dispensing cash seems to make an authentic relationship difficult if not impossible. I also have earned a reputation as a soft-touch. Some mornings at the laundromat, as many as three people may hit me up. At times like that, I wish I had an invisibility cloak.

My attitude varies. I respond more easily when a supplicant has his or her hand out in inclement weather. Runners and peace vigilers know well the potential fierceness of the elements. Like most people, my heart also goes out to handicapped, pregnant, very old, or very young beggars. Sometimes I see a person pushing a shopping cart full of their possessions in the snow or huddling for shelter under a bridge, and I take the initiative to offer help.

Then again, some characters push my buttons. I find one such fellow, a tall black man with a thick Jamaican accent, irksome. Like the street beggars in India, if he feels I didn't give him enough, he begs for more and always laughs when I give in. When I pulled up to the laundry yesterday morning, I saw him at the door to the adjoining Dunkin' Donuts. I rushed inside hoping he wouldn't see me, but no such luck.

As I put my first load in the washer, he tapped me on the shoulder and said, "I need two dollars."

Against my principles, I replied, "Not today. I have four loads of laundry to do."

This was true but deceptive. I also had more than thirty bucks in my pocket.

After imploring, "Come on, man," he drifted back outside.

Rather than watching the clothes swirling around in the machines, I like to read the *Worcester Telegram & Gazette* at a table in the Dunkin' Donuts. Interestingly, I do not buy anything and have never been asked to leave like those two black guys at a Starbucks in Philadelphia. Heck, I've never seen the employees ask men who are sound asleep to leave, although the staff does get grinchy at times about opening the bathrooms.

I hadn't read three sentences from the front page before the Jamaican guy plopped down opposite me, pointed to the back page, and demanded, "Let me see the horoscope."

"You read the horoscope?" I asked in surprise.

"Sometimes," he replied, as I gave him that section of the paper.

He read slowly out loud:

Don't feel you have to pay for someone else's mistake. Offer suggestions but don't physically or financially step in and take over. Personal changes can be made so long as they are within your budget.

What do you know? He's an Aquarius.

As one who never reads the horoscope, I felt moved to hear him do it. I reached into my pocket, gave him two dollar bills, and said, "Here's something for your budget."

His parting smile seemed more genuine than usual. For once, he didn't laugh at me.

The rest of the day unrolled as a typical Tuesday: house cleaning, going to the peace vigil, answering mail, writing, reading, and washing dishes. I welcomed a returning guest, Denise, who had been sleeping outside in what she described as "the freezing cold." No sign of my quarry. Yes, I admit curiosity has overcome anxiety, and I've actually started peering at everyone's left hand.

Due to a persistent and dull pain in my right hip, I emailed Karen:

> I took the day off. I'm not a runner anymore. I'm a fraud, a failure, a regular Dan Ford [another of my rivals]. My only chance for redemption is to run tomorrow morning. The forecast calls for showers until eight A.M., then light rain until nine, and then rain, some of it quite heavy until eight P.M. Can you run early? We don't need to do more than six miles to call ourselves runners? I could do six at six. What do you say?

Unfortunately, Karen shares an email address with her husband John, another trash-talking rival, who emailed me back: "You're right. You are not a runner."

John, a genuinely fast runner, joined Karen, me, and tens of thousands of others for the broiling hot 2011 Boston Marathon. Due to an injury, he stopped at thirteen miles. Karen did not tease him about the fact that she finished the race and he did not, but she did wear her finisher's medal for several days while John had to endure the ridicule of another runner who sent John a mock half marathon medal. The entire fiasco convinced John that the marathon was not for him, a conclusion that contributed to why he does not train with Karen.

John wears many hats. He is not only a runner but also a softball coach at Abby Kelley Foster Charter School. In a spirit of Christian charity, I replied to his remark that I am not a runner, "I see in today's paper that Abby Kelley got walloped in softball. I think they are a talented team that would go farther with the right coach."

As H. L. Mencken said, "Every normal man must be tempted, at times, to spit on his hands, hoist the black flag, and begin slitting throats," but I am more than able to cool that urge with choice words.

Karen's obstinate refusal to rise early dashed my hope to run before the deluge. She insisted that we run at 3:45 P.M. instead. If we can trust the Weather Channel (that's a big if), there was a good chance we'd drown before completing three miles, much less the six we needed.

By the way, before I forget (a more and more common occurrence), Barbara Roberts told me at the vigil that she and her husband watched all of the *Midsomer Murders*[39] British television series.

"You can always tell on that show when someone is about to get killed," she said. "The person looks at someone off camera and says, 'Oh, hello,' and, immediately afterwards, gets stabbed, drowned, shot, strangled, pushed off a roof, or, worst of all, set on fire."

Speaking of calamities, the front-page headline of Tuesday's paper announced: "Notre Dame Demolition Set to Begin." Barring some last-minute miracle, the wrecking ball will swing on Monday morning. If my mysterious informant had waited a week, we would have met in rubble under the stars.

I wonder what became of him. All I really know is that he was a solidly built, clean shaven, white guy in a Boston Celtics jacket. He sounded like a native Worcesterite, with an accent that cannot be faked. Nothing is funnier than watching British actor Benedict Cumberbatch trying to approximate a Boston accent in the movie, *Black Mass*[40]. Mayor Quimby on the *Simpsons*[41] comes closer than Sherlock did. Although I must admit that Jennifer Lawrence, in *American Hustle*[42,] (a movie filmed largely in Worcester, don'tcha know), did a pretty good New Jersey accent. If she had just a bit more coaching, she would have won best supporting actress, but the sky's the limit when an actor learns to drop those rs at the end of words.

Before I indulge in additional speculation about the Lazarus of The Dive Bar, I beg you to indulge me about a different creature that lives on after you're sure you've killed it—the dandelion. That cheerful flower of my youth, left to its own devices, will strangle a lawn. WikiHow says you can kill dandelions by blotting out the sun, smothering them with super-potent vinegar, burning the flowers with a blow torch (I'm not kidding), dousing them three times a day with boiling water, or digging each plant up by the roots. The labor-intensive latter option succeeds best, but still carries no guarantee, since even the smallest plant can have roots fatter than my thumb and deeper than the Marianas Trench. Assuming you got every dandelion out of your lawn is like trusting a surgeon to get every last micron of cancer out of a patient. Come this time of year, if I'm not out in our small yard every other day on my hands and knees attacking dandelion plants with remorseless vigor, their deceptively cheerful flowers bloom, turn downy white, and disperse millions of seeds.

I'm ashamed to admit that, as a child, I helped those villains along by plucking them, puffing up my cheeks, and blowing the seeds hither and yon. Yes, it's true. I am a reformed weed collaborator. It's bad enough that I have to apologize all the time for my gender, religion, race, and nation's past and present policies without having to self-identify as a one-time enabler of an invasive plant. How many dandelions I will have to uproot to cleanse my soul is unclear. Given the uncanny knack of those yellow devils to live again after being killed, my task could be endless. Maybe I have to employ multiple tactics, just as the mad monk Rasputin had to be poisoned, stabbed, shot, and drowned before he would stay dead.

WBUR's program *On Point* covers three or four topics during hour-long weekday broadcasts. The stories have clear beginnings, middles, and ends. True to the program's moniker, Tom Ashbrook used to stay on point (at least until he got fired for creating an abusive work environment). You may have noticed that I'm no Tom Ashbrook, even though I do have a younger brother named Tom who once found a dead hiker in the White Mountains National Forest. My brother Chipper has only one kidney.

Yet, unlike the Colorado and Jordan rivers that dry up before they get there, I eventually flow to the sea. In this book, that salty enormity concerns the mystery of a man who supposedly passed away on Saturday and then passed by me on Monday night. With stick-to-itiveness, I must move on without delay.

I think it's time I broadened my mind. Perhaps I too hastily accepted my informant's premise that Red Hand is a reanimated corpse. After all, I have no proof anyone actually got killed. The incident may have never occurred at all. The victim may not have expired. Despite my informant's skepticism, the object of my perplexity may in fact be a twin or, better yet, a clone. If he and his siblings were clones or triplets, that would make multiple sightings much less weird. Since I saw him driving a car, I have to rule out the possibility that he is a hologram, something I could not do if Tesla gets its way on self-driving cars.

While I'm at it, why not consider that I may be contending with numerous men, or even women, in clever disguises with lick-and-stick phony birthmark tattoos? Then we have spies, pranksters, aliens, angels, super heroes, super villains, mutants, replicants, cyborgs, robots, demons, ghosts, wizards, conjurers, and magicians to rule out. The more I think about it, the less significant it was that I saw the same man twice in two days.

Friday, April 27

This morning was a doozy! I left my house at 3:15 a.m. to begin the week's baking. When I pulled into the Phelan Center parking lot, I felt pleased to see that the building did not inexplicably blaze with lights. I did not feel pleased to find the main door unlocked. Since we have not locked our front door at the Catholic Worker since we opened in 1987, you would think the circumstance wouldn't disturb me. Yet, in the dead of night (there's that expression again), I'd rather not consider that someone entered the building before me.

So, I locked the door behind me as I entered, turned on the landing light, passed through the double doors to my right, turned on the hall light, entered the small downstairs kitchen, turned on its light, and gathered yeast, buttermilk, eggs, and carrots from the fridge. I retraced my steps, turning off lights behind me, and climbed to the second floor, turning on lights before me. I crossed the gym and unlocked the door to our bakery kitchen.

As I started preparing carrot raisin bran muffins, I thought I heard a noise. After pausing for a moment and hearing nothing more, I went back to work. From time to time, the basement furnace emits a loud bang, just as our convection oven sometimes does. I suspect both sounds derive from heat expanding metal. With no audible follow up, I added yeast and sugar to warm water for Italian bread. While I waited for that mixture to froth, I put six teaspoons of yeast into another bucket with oats, molasses, honey, and warm water. As I grabbed another bucket for a honey wheat dough, I heard a loud clang from the floor below me.

That clatter demanded investigation. Several years ago, on a night when I wasn't baking, someone broke into the building, ransacked closets, and stole audio-visual equipment. Blessed Sacrament rents us baking space at a very low rate. It behooves Claire and me to be good stewards of the property when we are around.

Having said that, I also realize the fact that virtually everyone who goes out to investigate a noise in a horror movie or novel suffers a terrible fate. On the other hand, in the urban legend *The Boyfriend in the Car*[43], when a couple runs out of gas and the boyfriend goes to get help, the girl hears a yell and then scratching on the car's roof. Too terrified to investigate, she learns in the morning when the police arrive that some wild beast waylaid her boyfriend, later found thrown up in a tree branch just above the car. His throat cut in such a way that he could not speak, he tried to get her attention by reaching down to the roof with the tips of his fingers. Because she did not open the car doors and look outside, he bled to death. On the other hand, in the urban Legend, *The Hook*[44], a couple takes off just as a murderer reaches to open their car door.

As I've said previously, if I am screwed, I'm screwed. Nothing I do or don't do can effect a different outcome. Although I have been arrested more than forty times for civil disobedience, I have never gotten away with breaking Murphy's Law.

Back to the clatter downstairs, I boldly set out, long flat spatula in hand, to investigate. I left the bright kitchen, passed through the dark gym and brightly lit landing down to the first floor, where I made certain the front door remained locked. Then I turned to the heavy double doors, opened them, turned on the lights, and inspected the rooms one by one. I found no one in the supply closet, the small or large meeting rooms, bathrooms, janitor's tiny office, or kitchenette. By then, I had so many lights on that the Center could probably be seen from outer space.

Only one spot remained uninspected: the boiler room. While the rest of the building is neat and modern, the Phelan Center's energy center could easily pass for the engine room on the *Titanic*. It would not surprise me at all to see barechested laborers shoveling coal into the furnace. The door to that inferno, reinforced with iron bands and steel bolts, virtually screamed, "Don't open me, you fool!" And yet, I did (the difference between a hero and an idiot devolves from the better luck of the former).

I flicked the switch only to see a light more suggested than actual. I had surmised as much. After all, Morlocks[45], which lurk underground, cannot abide brightness.

I took one step inside and whispered, "Is anyone in here?"

As with all rhetorical questions, I did not utter it to elicit a response.

"So far, so good," I thought as I stepped down the short flight of concrete stairs. "Ally, ally, outs in free. Come out, come out, wherever you are," I called a tiny bit louder,

Still nothing.

Thank you, Jesus.

I ducked to avoid some pipes and peeked around what looked like a nineteenth-century boiler and saw nothing more remarkable than a dusty floor and mysterious monitoring devices mounted on the walls.

While I had hardly inspected every inch, I'd seen enough to conclude that the room I stood in harbored no intruders.

"Fine by me," I murmured to myself as I reversed my steps and doused light after light, Unfortunately, when I opened the double doors, to my shock, darkness greeted me. Although I had turned them on only moments before, neither the first-floor landing, stairway, nor second-floor landing lights were on.

"Please let it be a blown fuse," I muttered while reaching for the first switch. To my eternal gratitude the landing light went on.

It could only mean that someone had turned the lights off behind me. Someone at 3:30 A.M. Someone now between me and my rising doughs.

Considering my discombobulated memory, it was possible I had thrown the switches behind me, but I doubted that very much. So I opened and rechecked the lock on the outside door, flicked the switch on the stairway lights, climbed the steps slowly, and illuminated the second landing. The empty cooling racks still sat there along with the boxes of twist ties, labels, and bags. Nothing amiss.

As I entered the empty gym, I could see the kitchen light out as well. Since I had searched everywhere else, the kitchen remained the only place anyone hiding in the building could be. The best-case scenario I could imagine meant bumping into someone like Eddy, an affable homeless guy who can sleep soundly on a sidewalk. Although often incontinent, Eddy wouldn't assault me, and I'd much rather deal with him than an assailant.

When I poked my head into the kitchen, I saw absolutely nothing save the red glow of the stove burners I had left on to help the doughs rise. I flicked the light switch up and down several times and got a brief spark before all went dark again. In that flash of light, which could not have been more than a second, I thought I saw someone standing back to me behind the stainless-steel table by the oven. However, when I flipped the switch again and the lights came on normally, there was no one beside me in the room. A card-carrying member of The Amalgamated Cowards of America Union, I surprised myself by turning the lights on and off again once more to be sure.

I was absolutely alone.

Several explanations for the phenomenon come to mind. When a person in the dark experiences a flash of light, a black spot often appears in the viewer's center of vision. In my semi-hysterical state, I was certainly vulnerable to suggestion. An imaginative person could spin a black spot into an intruder with long greasy hair, fists clenched at his side, and wearing a black overcoat (not that I paid much attention).

Another possibility, also perfectly reasonable in my case, is that I suffered from a straight-out hallucination. While snorkeling off the coast of the Puerto Rican Island of Vieques, my son Justin swears he saw a manta ray. Although diving right next to him, I saw nothing and believe that he saw what he wanted to see.

My last hypothesis doesn't much reassure me. One of the hard lessons I learned while tangling with the Prince of Darkness back in 1978 (pp. 12-28 in *Nothing Is Impossible*) involves the fact that Evil-with-a-capital-E prefers anonymity. As C.S. Lewis tells us in *The Screwtape Letters*[46], there is no greater advantage in the Devil's war to corrupt humanity than our disbelief in Evil. The upside of the demonic preference for covert warfare is that those who let sleeping devils lie never have to meet them face to face.

The reality of demons has no bearing. A person who gets him or herself worked up enough to imagine seeing a hellish legionnaire is just as frightened as someone who actually sees one. A skeptic likely shrugs off everything short of a kiss on the lips from Lucifer. Ignorance is very much a state of bliss.

In 1978, I enjoyed idyllic days and nights when I resolved to ignore the possibility of Evil. When I opened my mind even a crack to its existence, lights went out and on at will, noises came from nowhere, and I got chills down my spine. I don't want that to happen again—especially not eight days before the marathon.

So, I took my own advice and focused on making the best Irish soda, oatmeal raisin, and honey wheat bread I could. In less than two hours, my heart rate returned almost to normal.

At 5:30, with breads safely tucked in the oven, I slipped away to put four loads of our guests' laundry into washing machines. I found a nickel and two pennies on the floor, and I took them as good omens.

I had forty-five minutes before I had to return to the bakery, so I bought the Worcester *Telegram & Gazette* and sat down to read it. Headlines like "EPA chief tries to divert blame for ethics woes," "Mike Pompeo sworn in," and "Public colleges consider fee increase," while not comforting, did not qualify as apocalyptic. The Bucks forced the Celtics into game seven. *Harry Potter*[47] is now appearing on Broadway. *The Avengers*[48] have returned for their millionth sequel. Dagwood and Blondie are still going strong after more than fifty years of marriage.

Nothing struck me as remarkable, so I set the paper aside and checked the laundry. The first machine had five more minutes, so I opened the paper again to the obituaries or, as my friend Elizabeth Mullaney calls them, "The Irish Sports Page."

More and more often, I find death notices for people I know, and sometimes I am moved to tears or laughter by words that surviving relatives choose to print. I only wish that the writers would be more explicit about the causes of death. Euphemisms like "passed away peacefully in his home" do not help me realistically confront mortality. Even though my only experience with corpses occurred in war zones, I am still pretty sure death is wicked hard no matter how it happens.

Then I saw it at the bottom of the page on the right—an obituary with the photo of the man I met at Notre Dame Church. It was definitely him, no doubt about it.

I pulled the paper closer and read:

WORCESTER — Donald M. Banes, 34 of Worcester, MA, passed away unexpectedly on Tuesday, April 17. He leaves behind a sister Nancy Healy of Webster, MA, and many friends at the Worcester Boys & Girls Club. Born at Saint Vincent Hospital in Worcester, Donald was a standout basketball player for South High, who went on to earn a bachelor's degree in Social Work from Quinsigamond Community College.

A funeral Mass will be celebrated on Monday, April 30 at 10 a.m. in Saint John's Church on 44 Temple Street in Worcester. Burial will follow in Hope Cemetery. Calling hours will be held Sunday from 6-8 P.M. in O'Connor Brothers Funeral Home, 592 Park Avenue.

In lieu of flowers, memorial donations may be made to Saint Xavier Center, care of Saint John's, or The Mustard Seed Catholic Worker, 93 Piedmont Street, Worcester, MA 01609.

Yikes, at times like this, I sure do wish I had a sidekick.

Sunday, April 29

A pale, red-headed woman in an Insane Clown Posse[49] sweatshirt opened the door for me at the laundromat. It really was too early to chat with a courteous "juggala" of the psychopathic hip hop band, so I merely said, "Thanks."

I found four pennies and a quarter on the floor, on top of the machines, and in a change slot, bringing Claire's and my retirement fund up to $79.93, a good omen for what promised to be a busy day.

As Claire headed out to Prince of Peace Church in Princeton (where else would it be?) to sell our bread, I readied myself for an eight-mile run with Karen, who insisted that our marathon taper required the glacial pace of ten minutes a mile. To take my mind off the fact that we moved only slightly faster than the slow-motion Brits on the beach in the opening scene of *Chariots of Fire*[50], I reviewed aloud the last few entries of this journal. While she certainly had no interest in partnering with me in the investigation, Karen agreed to be a sounding board, especially if it meant keeping an easy pace. The mystery intrigued her, but she didn't offer a theoretical solution. I agreed with her that we need more data.

To that end, I pledged to visit The Dive Bar in the afternoon and afterwards attend Donald Banes's wake. The time has come for me to go on the offensive. I can't just wait around for clues to drop out of the sky.

By the way, as I prepared for Saturday's race at Worcester State University, I took extra care not to make any more bobbleheaded mistakes—like forgetting my shorts. At the weekly 5K, some time back, Kevin Ducharme, a pretty fast high school runner, had to stop mid race to tie his shoes. Six years ago, during a rainy WSU 5K, I experienced the same misfortune. It's a newbie mistake and costs a runner dearly. Forgetting my watch is another snafu that discombobulates me. Leaving my hat at home exposes my bald head to deadly cancer-causing rays. Forgetting my shirt scuttles the run entirely. There's no way, no matter how hot the day, that this Irish Catholic will run shirtless, especially not after seeing how that approach earned someone the nickname Flabby Dan. I checked off stretching, putting Vaseline on areas prone to blisters, and emptying my bladder as well as remembering to bring two Susan B. Anthony dollars and two Kennedy halves to pay for the race. All systems were go. I double-tied my laces for insurance.

As I prepared to depart, I stood with hands on my hips in the doorway to the kitchen and proclaimed to Claire, "Behold, the complete runner!"

She glanced at my feet and shook her head sadly. When I looked down, I realized that I had on two different colored shoes.

Once I made an adjustment, I packed copies of *Murder on Mott Street* and set out. You never know when you might make a sale.

"I'm working on a new book," I announced to Bill, Dave, Vin, Valerie, and Carlos. "For five dollars, I'll promise to include you in it, and for twenty dollars, I'll leave you out."

Vin immediately started to pull Andrew Jackson out of his wallet.

"No, no, Vin," I said waving off the proffered cash. "Your money is no good here. I wouldn't think of writing a book without you in it."

Back to Sunday. Storytelling indeed slowed me down. Our first five miles clocked at 9:52, but, after that, I renewed my typically noisy style of breathing, something other runners hear from a quarter of a mile. Besides annoying anyone within earshot, my sounds-like-an-I'm-dying technique for enriching my blood with oxygen causes me to run faster.

Despite her protestations to the contrary, Karen flew along in my wake. We finished with an average pace of 9:38 and 9 flat for the final two miles. More important, we both felt good. If we can only avoid the many land mines that could still derail us in next Sunday's marathon, we will set personal records. That's a mighty big if. Things as small as a splinter or sore throat are as good as a dagger. We will have to tread very lightly this week. God willing, I won't have to wrestle the red-handed man.

Therefore, with caution in mind, in the early afternoon, I set out for The Dive Bar at the corner of Temple and Green streets in a part of Worcester now known as the Canal District. Irish immigrants built the referenced canal from Worcester to the Narragansett Bay in the 1830s. The waterway supplemented the mostly unnavigable Blackstone River, but lost its economic viability with construction of much faster railway lines.

Only a few sections of the canal remain exposed today, none of them in Worcester. While Providence, Rhode Island's former mayor, Buddy Cianci, transformed the canal's terminus into a tourist attraction, proposals to uncover and develop the canal hereabouts lie fallow. Yet, while flowing water amounts merely to an idea in Worcester nowadays, flowing cash does not. The Canal District hums with development. The restoration of Union Station in 1999, a building once called "a poem in stone," preceded transformation of several brick mills into apartments, the opening of restaurants and bars, and construction of a hockey rink, intermodal transportation hub, hotels, a courthouse, and hundreds of units of housing. The rejuvenated downtown attracts new residents and visitors from around New England and beyond.

Back in the early twentieth century, Water Street, two blocks east of The Dive, was the heart of an immigrant Jewish community. Jewish bakeries, in particular, thrived. Until the last of them closed several years ago, Water Street thronged on Sunday mornings with lots of Christians coming down after church to buy bagels and other baked goods. Weintraub's Deli remains Water Street's only vestige of Jewish presence, which largely shifted to Worcester's more affluent West Side.

In the West Side neighborhood, they founded numerous synagogues, including Temple Emmanuel, attended by the anti-Vietnam war, environmental activist and anarchist Abbie Hoffman. Claire and I went to his funeral in 1989. After the Temple Emanuel congregation merged with Temple Sinai on Salisbury Street to become Temple Emanuel Sinai, the former temple became the property of Worcester State University and, for three years, the registration site for our Saturday 5K races. Small world.

Each September, Fiddler's Green Hibernian Club, a pub and function center located behind The Dive Bar on Temple Street, hosts The Canal Digger's 5K, which draws more than a thousand people. Claire and I never miss running it. Vin and I have had many an epic battle on that course. My older brother

Mike and former marathon coach, Rich Larsen, who says I am uncoachable, take part each year. After the run, pizza, Table Talk pies, oranges, beer, Irish music, and prizes abound.

In my college days, Green Street featured eight blue-collar bars where you could get a draught beer for fifty cents. Even then, the area had distinct charm. Sir Morgan's Cove, a bar that could hold barely seventy people, hosted The Rolling Stones for a free concert in 1981. Claire and I saw Jonathan Richman of The Modern Lovers perform there in 2006. Green Street's string of bars continued across Kelley Square on Millbury Street and into Polish and then Irish neighborhoods. You could buy kielbasa during the day and hear Irish music at the Tiperrary Pub at night. Everyone knew Steeple Bumsteads as a good place for parties and brawls. Behind the businesses on either side of the street stood rows of triple decker houses. The culturally vibrant and lively, if rundown, area thrived.

Churches also defined the neighborhood. Saint John's, the oldest Catholic Church in Worcester, is across the street from Fiddler's Green. Originally an Irish parish, it now hosts a diverse community and a lively pastor, Father John Madden, a classmate of mine from Holy Cross College and former volunteer at Saint Joseph's Catholic Worker in New York City. Just to the southeast you can still attend Mass said in Polish at Our Lady of Częstochowa. Notre Dame, which received a temporary stay from the wrecking ball earlier this week, served French-Canadians. When I came here as a freshman in 1976, they called Worcester a "city of churches, banks, and bars." To this day in Worcester, you can attend Mass on any given Sunday in seven languages.

The Dive Bar both fits into that history and stands out. For eight months in 2013 and 2014, it hosted our Monday night runs and potluck. In summer, it was wonderful because The Dive sports a lovely "beer garden" out back, a fenced-in space with hops growing all around, comfortable tables, and, oftentimes, free live music. Gone is the day when every Green Street bar featured cheap lager. The Dive presents new craft beers with so much regularity that it has acquired a reputation for excellence among beer-drinking aficionados. During our weekly sojourn there, I found a brew called "The Beer of the Gods" particularly enjoyable, even though it cost eight dollars a mug.

Of course, no establishment that calls itself a dive bar coddles its customers. The narrow place has only small tables, stools, and a long bar. Illuminated mainly by strings of Christmas lights, small opaque windows facing Green Street, and a cracked porthole in the door, The Dive is pretty dark. To point out the roughness of the tiny bathroom would be like mentioning the wetness of Niagara Falls.

After Claire returned from Prince of Peace and departed for her run, I left Saints Francis and Thérèse house and went north on Mason Street and right on Chandler all the way to Kelley Square. I turned left onto Green Street and parked just past the Restaurant Superstore where we get most of our baking supplies, including cool oven mitts.

I opened The Dive's door with its nautical window and took a seat at the bar. After checking the blackboard, I ordered the least expensive brew I could find, the Mystic Table Beer, from Chelsea, Massachusetts. I recognized none of the sixteen beer offerings. The Finback Whale Farm IPA, for example, costs three dollars more and, according to the label, has twice as much kick as Mystic Table. I didn't dare risk it but wondered nonetheless.

I saw only three other people beside me inside: a woman with a nose ring, jet black hair, leather vest, and jeans; a male biker in standard biker attire; and a clean-cut twenty-something guy in a suit with loosened tie. Music played, but I couldn't place it.

Behind the bar, a poster advertised an event on October 26:

> For your listening pleasure we present to you . . .
> Big-Eyed Rabbit! Take a barrelhouse rhythm section laying
> down a bed of gravel to kick your vices in. Pair that with
> a man so infatuated and saturated with "Hill Country
> Blues" and then press thru a meat grinder. The result is one
> Big-Eyed Rabbit.

Although I read it twice, I still had little idea what kind of music it would be save blues. By the way, I sure do miss Gilrein's Home of Blues on Main Street. That was a hopping place where you could wear sunglasses indoors and fit right in. In the bar's confines, Claire and I danced many a night to wild saxophone and harmonica. On the corner of Austin and High streets, The Hottentot featured Billie Holiday, BB King, Willie Dixon, and Muddy Waters. It closed just before I moved to town in 1976 but, thanks be to God, Claire and I did once get to see BB King from the balcony of the Palladium on Main Street. More recently, Aiden dragged me to the Palladium to see Apocalyptica, a super long-haired Danish screamo band that plays electric cellos. They made the concerts I saw by Jethro Tull and Blondie seem pretty tame, but I continue to believe a show I saw by The Talking Heads tops them all.

While I pondered my sad withdrawal from the music scene, the bartender set down a pint of my mysterious beer. Golden yellow with a white head and frosty cold, it had a light taste with a slight hint of citrus.

"What do you think?" the barkeep asked.

"I like it," I replied in all honesty. "I have to admit, though, I'm not overly fond of the high-alcohol beers."

He nodded before moving down to the other end of the bar to serve the biker.

I took out a copy of the *Telegram's* obit and placed it on the bar. When I had finished two-thirds of my drink, the bartender came over and asked if I wanted another.

"No, thanks," I answered while turning the obit in his direction, "but I was wondering if you remembered this fellow."

"Sure," he said. "I didn't know his name, but I saw him in here several times. He seemed like a nice guy. I'm sorry to hear he died."

"I am, too. His name was Don Banes," I said. "Do you remember him being here a couple of Saturdays ago?"

Resting his arms on the bar and leaning slightly closer to me, he replied, "Actually, I do remember because another guy got in his face."

"A middle-aged guy with a red birthmark on his left hand?" I asked.

"As a matter of fact, yes," he noted with some surprise.

"Can you tell me about what happened? I would really appreciate knowing."

"Sure," he confided. "Banes came in and sat at the bar next to the birth-marked customer, who was lecturing a millennial wearing a March-for-Our-Lives sweatshirt."

"What do you mean?" I asked.

"Well, I don't know how the exchange started, but I did overhear the older dude saying the NRA and gun industry are too cozy with the government for any real reform."

"When the kid said he thought that things would be different after the Parkland massacre, the geezer unleashed a torrent of statistics to prove him wrong."

"And Banes got angry about that?" I asked.

"No. He couldn't help but hear their exchange, but he seemed to be minding his own business. At least that was the case until the old guy started ripping into the naiveté of people who believe in the possibility of either social or personal change. That pissed Banes off enough to butt in to say he knew from experience that people can overcome adversity.

The old guy turned to Banes and said, "Anecdotal examples don't change the fundamental fact that those born at the bottom generally die there." Without even waiting for Banes to reply, he turned back to the anti-gun kid, but Banes wasn't so easily brushed off, so he tapped the dude on the shoulder. Before Banes could say a word, though, the dude suggested they resolve their differences outside, something Banes readily agreed to."

"Weren't you worried about trouble?" I asked.

"Kind of," the bartender said, "but neither of them was drunk, and the old guy wasn't just talking off the top of his head. He quoted independent studies and surveys. He seemed like some kind of expert or college professor, not a brawler, but, a few minutes later, just to be on the safe side, I looked out front and saw they both were gone. That's the last I've seen of them."

"Thanks so much," I said after leaving a tip and heading home.

Two hours later, I found myself in a much brighter but less cheerful locale—O'Connor's Funeral Home on Park Avenue. While many New England mortuaries operate out of stately Victorian homes, O'Connor's is a low-to-the-ground, ranch-style, relatively modern building fronted by a treeless lawn and backed by a parking lot. Not far from two excellent Vietnamese restaurants and another Dunkin' Donuts, O'Connor's was the site of the funeral of my sixty-nine-year-old friend Nick Kanaracus in July of 2016. A former president of Central Mass Striders and graduate of South High, where I coach cross country, Nick was an avid runner. He finished more than forty marathons and was working with his friend Bob Dio to run all five hundred miles of Worcester's streets a bit at a time over the course of a single year when cancer suddenly struck him down. Bob, a deacon at Saint Peter's Church, succeeded Nick as the Striders' president. Bob used to be my assistant coach at South. Even though he's nearly eighty, Bob drives a convertible as if Worcester's streets were his own personal race track. Once again, I digress.

After signing the guest register in O'Connor's carpeted and paneled reception area, I filed into a room designated for Don Banes's wake. About twenty people sat in four rows of chairs facing an open coffin flanked by tall candles and flowers on the sides and a velvet-covered kneeler in front. Small windows let in warm sunlight.

It made a very different impression from Graham Putnam & Mahoney Funeral Parlor on Main Street, which held the wakes of at least two of our guests. Although jammed in a space across from a Family Dollar, Pennywise Market, a car dealership, and other businesses, Graham Putnam evokes a different era. I can easily imagine an ebony, horse-drawn hearse with a driver in a top hat pulling up to the porte-cochère.

The owner and chief mortician at Graham Putnam, Peter Stefan, has long handled dignified funerals for the indigent. He affords the same respect for those he buries in unmarked graves as for those with pricy granite monuments. His integrity was on national display in 2013 when he was the only funeral director willing to accept the body of Tamerlan Tsarnaev, the mastermind of the Boston Marathon bombing that took three lives, including that of eight-year-old Martin Richards. As a runner who crossed the finish line on Boylston Street with my son Aiden only two minutes before the first of the two explosions, I remember well that terrible day as well as the highly militarized response to it by local and national law enforcement. Claire and I saw armored vehicles on the Boston Common the following morning. Emotions ran very high. Although no runners were injured, all of us were affected. For the first time in my life, I witnessed here at home the kind of senseless and indiscriminate violence of bombings I have seen overseas.

After Peter Stefan agreed to accept the body of Tsarnaev, a furious demonstration took place on Main Street with people carrying American flags and signs which read, "Do Not

Bury Him on US Soil" and "It's a Disgrace to Our Military." Online comments were more forceful: "Send his carcass to his homeland. Let them dispose of it." and "He murdered and maimed innocent Americans. He does not have the right to be buried on American soil." and "The only 'peace' he deserves is a 'piece' of the ocean bottom."

The next day, with a sign that said, "Burying the Dead is a Work of Mercy," I stood opposite the funeral parlor beside the angry protesters. Contrary to the shouting match that one might expect in such circumstance, I had a good conversation with two opponents who ended up switching their positions. Clearly, their initial response was more emotional than rational.

In an appeal Claire and I sent out for people to support Mr. Stefan, we wrote, "No matter what kind of life someone lived, morticians take a solemn oath to provide them a decent burial. Those who work at Graham Putnam & Mahoney have done this for some of Worcester's poorest and least popular citizens for years. Theirs was the only funeral home which would bury the victims of AIDs in the early days of that epidemic."

A diverse group of more than forty people, including a number of students from Clark University, turned out to support Mr. Stefan. One of the attendees, Sister Rena Mae Gagnon, a member of the Little Franciscans of Mary and our friend, told the press, "I was saddened by the initial reaction when I heard people were here protesting. We're Christians. We're not to act that way."

Another friend, Clarence Burley, clerk for the Worcester Friends Meeting, said, "The violence that was in Tamerlan has left his body, which is a temple of the Holy Spirit."

Holy Cross College professor Vickie Langohr, who lives in Watertown where authorities apprehended the younger Tsarnaev, held a sign that read, "Human Rights Are for All Humans." Worcesterite Douglas Medina's placard proclaimed, "We are Proud of Graham Putnam & Mahoney." He told reporters, "Tsarnaev is no longer able to hurt us. I am not condoning what he did, but he has to be buried."

Ultimately, a groundswell of support rose for Peter Stefan, who has since received many honors. The episode spoke to me of the powerful ability of a compassionate community to quell rage.

When I took a seat in the back row at O'Connor's, I saw none of the controversy that surrounded Tsarnaev's burial. At Don Banes's low-key wake, people came in, knelt in front of the coffin, offered sympathy to the bereaved family, sat for a few minutes, and departed. From my vantage point, I couldn't see visible signs of violence on the corpse. Then again, I imagine the mortician obscured them or would have insisted on a closed casket. I assumed the middle-aged couple clad in black standing next to the coffin to be Banes's sister and brother-in-law. Their sorrowful demeanor and solemn venue made it clear it would be inappropriate to pump them for information about their dead relative.

Thankfully, Barbara Lucci filed in. A longtime friend and tireless worker for the Homeless Outreach Advocacy Project, Barbara seeks out the hard-core, longtime homeless, wins their trust, and coaxes them off the street and into decent housing. She's the real deal. Some of our most colorful guests came to us via Barbara, including a woman with an adorable little dog and another who hadn't taken a bath in two years.

A devout Catholic, Barbara works with a vigorous campaign to prevent the demolition of Worcester's flagship Italian church, Our Lady of Mount Carmel, less than a mile from Notre Dame. She paid her respects and sat down beside me.

"Hi, Scott. How are you?" she asked.

"I'm fine, Barbara," I replied. "How did you know Donald?"

"He had a drug-addicted younger brother who, despite his family's and my best efforts, died on the street. Unlike most people, though, Don wasn't bitter. He worked hard to make sure others didn't end up like his brother."

"In what way?" I inquired.

"He was a powerhouse at the Boys & Girls Club. He also coached youth basketball at Saint Peter's and volunteered some overnights at Saint John's shelter the last two winters. His death will hit a lot of people hard."

"Yowser," I said. "Do you know how he died? The paper just said it was unexpected."

"I heard he had a heart attack while waiting for a Greyhound bus," she said. "How did you know him?"

"I didn't really," I admitted. "I only met him last week, and then BOOM. I read in the *T&G* that he was dead. It kind of shocked me."

"No matter how many wakes I attend," she said, "death always throws me for a loop."

The more I think about it, the more I agree with her.

Monday, April 30

Today did not begin well. After the usual house chores, I set out to deliver copies of *Murder on Mott Street* to two professors at Holy Cross, Predrag Cicovaki in peace studies and Maria Rodrigues in sociology.

To facilitate the outing, I had written down their office hours and addresses. When I arrived at the college, I went into Stein Hall but had forgotten the sheet of paper with the room numbers. I remembered that one was 327 and the other, 518, so I took the elevator up to the third floor only to discover I was in the wrong department. So I jumped back in the elevator, went up to the fifth floor, and got similarly frustrated. It all mystified me until I realized that Predrag's office is in Smith, not Stein.

I trotted over to Smith 327, which I also had incorrect and then to 518. While that is indeed Predrag's office, he holds hours on Tuesday not Monday, and with no secretary around, I couldn't leave my book.

Miffed, I sought Maria's office in the sociology department in O'Kane only to learn that Maria teaches political science. I was on the wrong floor in the wrong building. But God took pity on me, and I managed to leave my book with her secretary. Unfortunately, as soon as I got home, I found an old email from Maria asking me to deliver two books, not one. Blizzards of incompetence like that convince me that I had better rush the manuscript for this book before I become a full-time idiot.

Lest you think this escapade results from advancing age, I must admit that, after my first visit to Holy Cross in 1976, I drove back to my parent's house in their great big LTD sedan when I had a blowout. I pulled over safely to change the tire, successfully jacked up the car, and removed the full-size spare tire from the trunk but could not for the life of me remove the lug nuts.

After a futile hour of my useless activity, a good Samaritan stopped and offered to help. I told him the lug nuts must have been put on with a screw gun because I couldn't budge them, but he removed them with ease, smiled at me, and said, "Righty tighty, lefty loosey."

I hoped for no screwups at the pub run. Since Karen insisted we should do only a one-mile warmup, I went to the Ballot Box Bar early and ran an extra mile by myself.

As I passed the Broadway and The Dive Bar, I reflected on what I had learned so far. What Barbara told me made sense of why Banes had confronted Mr. Red Hand at The Dive. Any person who works to save people from the hell on earth of drug addiction, especially someone whose own brother died of an overdose, would be furious to hear somebody dismiss the possibility of personal change. Despair can catapult addicts to suicide. Years ago, a relapsed heroin addict took his life a day after he left our house.

Taking away people's hope is monstrous.

Karen arrived just as I turned the corner back onto Water Street, so I joined her inside the Ballot Box, where Vin already sat at the bar chatting with Kelsey, the affable bartender, who also plays rugby on the same team with another of our runners named Killian. A minute later, Carlos came in followed by Mike Morrissey, Mark Favreault, and an Irish woman, Sarah Johnson, who plans to study at UMass Med School until the end of June. We set down the food for the potluck and got ready for the six P.M. warmup. Claire couldn't join us tonight because she had a celebration to attend with those who helped produce an informative and moving multi-media performance called *We Grow In Courage* about the women who bravely campaigned for civil rights in Mississippi and Alabama in the 1960s as members of the Student Nonviolent Coordinating Committee.

Two unfamiliar men came in, one about twenty-six and the other about fifty. The older guy hoped to recruit runners to join the Genesis Club team running the Falmouth Road Race in August. Genesis does terrific work with people who struggle with issues of mental health. The other man's name was Chris.

"Are you new?" I asked him.

"No," he replied. "I ran the course last year but have been away. Is it still the same?"

After saying that the route had not changed, I asked, "Where have you been?"

"Kabul," he replied without elaboration.

"Oh," I answered. "I've been to Kabul. I was there in 2011, and my wife was there in 2002." I didn't bother to say that we had both been there on peace missions. "I heard on the news that thirty-eight Afghan civilians were killed today, including ten journalists and eleven children."

"Yah," he said shaking his head. "There have been a number of terrible attacks lately."

"When I was there," I said, "people called Afghan President Karzai 'the mayor of Kabul' because that was all the territory he actually controlled."

He nodded.

"No one has been able to conquer Afghanistan—not Alexander the Great, the British, Russians, or the US," I continued.

"They call it the 'graveyard of empires,'" he agreed.

"Did you see the abandoned Russian tanks and artillery all along the Panjshir river valley north of Bagram?" I asked.

"No," he replied. "We used to be able to go out to markets, restaurants and the countryside, but, on this tour, they kept us pretty buttoned up. There's a great strip of highway near the airport that would be perfect for running, but they won't let us use it. The only upside I can see to this string of recent attacks against civilians is that it might be a sign that the insurgents are starting to fear the Afghan army."

"Maybe," I answered, "but my impression was that the poorly paid Afghan soldiers desert when attacked by the Taliban. Two of my brothers-in-law are Vietnam vets. They remember well how the South Vietnamese army melted away after we pulled out. We've already been in Afghanistan almost seventeen years. I think the Taliban will take over whenever we leave, even if we stay there another ten or twenty years."

To my surprise, he said, "You know, a third of the money allocated to pay Afghan troops is set aside for units that don't even exist. The money just disappears."

Before I could ask more about Afghan corruption, Karen announced it was time to run.

Tuesday, May 1

Today is May Day, the Feast of Saint Joseph the Worker, and the eighty-fifth anniversary of the founding of the Catholic Worker movement in New York City by Dorothy Day and Peter Maurin. Union members and their supporters rallied today in front of Worcester's city hall to call for a living wage and other measures of economic justice. Mayor Joe Petty, a real friend to immigrants, workers, and the poor, showed his support. It's nice to live in a diverse city with leaders against whom you don't feel compelled to protest.

No matter how good a society is, though, there will always be suffering. Our guest, Christine, went on a cleaning spree upstairs with absolute mania until she joined us at supper. Clearly, she was on something. Like many people we have had to confront about insobriety, she was defensive and accusatory. Claire offered to drive her to the hospital, but she insisted on taking her things and leaving on foot. All too often, pride prevents people from taking help.

In contrast, Denise asked me to give her a ride to the bank so she could take out some of her social security income. On the ride, she said, "You know, I'm dying."

"What do you mean?" I asked in surprise.

"I've got hepatitis B, and it's incurable," she replied. "I probably got it when my brother gave me a tattoo. Since then, I get exhausted even on short walks. My therapist told me there was an upside to it because now my name is at the top of the list for emergency housing. You know, they want $600 or $700 for a room. How can I afford that on a $750 check?"

Despite her trials, Denise was effusively grateful. She told me over and over how much she appreciated her stay at our house. When she came out of the bank, she insisted on paying me back five dollars she had borrowed last year. She also wanted me to give an envelope containing ten dollars to our guest Sean, who had given her a ride to get clothing, and another envelope with twenty-five dollars to "help out" our guest John, the one with the shamrock swastika.

While part of me wanted to convince Denise that she can't afford to give away any of her money, her unselfishness impressed another part of me. We'd live in a different world if everyone were so generous.

Wednesday, May 2

I went to the Broadway Diner this morning with the slim hope that someone might remember Mr. Red Hand from April 16. Given that the event occurred more than two weeks ago Sunday and that the place is especially busy on weekends, I was not optimistic.

For years, I have told my children and visitors that the Broadway occupies the same building that the famous anarchist Emma Goldman and her partner Alexander Berkman used as an ice cream parlor in 1892, but I now know that they actually occupied a storefront on nearby Winter Street. We used to have her quote on our bathroom wall: "If I can't dance, I don't want to be part of your revolution." While Goldman kept scooping ice cream, Berkman attempted to assassinate the robber baron Henry Clay Frick, for which he spent fourteen years in what *Hogan's Heroes*[51] called "the cooler."

Besides churches, banks, and bars, diners abound in Worcester. Several of them still operate in old railroad cars. A favorite place for my children and me to get French fries and grilled cheese sandwiches, the Miss Worcester Diner has done business on Southbridge Street since 1948. The National Register of Historic Places listed it in 2003.

A block away on Lamartine Street, the 1950s Corner Lunch Diner sports a shiny aluminum exterior and *Happy Days*[52] interior with brightly colored vinyl booths. As grown-ups, my kids prefer it over Miss Woo, the railcar's nickname in keeping with a sobriquet for the City of Worcester. The National Register also lists The Corner Lunch.

Each diner has a unique character. Take the Boulevard in Worcester's Little Italy, the Pickle Barrel on Pleasant, or Ralph's Chadwick Square Diner on Grove for examples. Open twenty-four hours, the Boulevard diner always serves bacon and eggs, eggplant Parmesan, and spaghetti and meatballs. The Pickle Barrel, a block away from our sister community The Mustard Seed Catholic Worker, offers fish and chips every Friday. Attached to a bar and dance club, Ralph's Chadwick Square Diner hosts some of the coolest bands. Most of my family had a great time there last year rocking to Jonathan Richman. Believe me when I tell you diners stand head and shoulders above any fast-food chain.

Located at the corner of Harrison and Water streets, the Broadway has a counter and a few tables in front and a larger room out back. Thirty friends and family enjoyed brunch in that room the day after our daughter Grace's wedding to the irrepressible Anthony Sliwoski.

Today, I took a seat at the counter and ordered an egg and cheese sandwich, a high cholesterol treat. The place was less than half full. When she seemed to have a moment, I asked the woman behind the counter if she had worked on the Sunday in question. She said she hadn't, but her partner down at the other end of the counter had.

They graciously traded places, and after introducing myself, I asked, "Do you remember a middle-aged white guy with a red birthmark on his left hand coming in here on Sunday the sixteenth?"

"You know," she confided, "unless someone is a regular, I usually wouldn't remember them, but that guy was an exception."

"Really?" I brightened. "In what way?"

"He sidled up to Arnie, who told me the day before he's having marital problems. I don't know if the guy with the birthmark knew it or not, but he went on about the inevitability of divorce. In no time, he had Arnie in tears. Finally, I had enough of it, gave him his check, and said, 'I think it's time you moved on.' The weird thing is, he didn't seem offended in the least. He dropped a fiver on the counter, grinned, and walked out like he'd just won the lottery instead of being given the bum's rush."

That must have been just before Banes saw him get into a cab. The jerk smiled at Banes too.

Thursday, May 3

When Karen called me yesterday, she said in a barely audible voice, "Can you believe this?"

The god who hates marathoners had inflicted her with laryngitis. Although she had no other adverse symptoms, she feared they would appear in time to screw up Sunday's race. I encouraged her as best as I could while panicking that I, too, would fall ill.

"I'll be good. I'll be good," I murmured to every imaginable deity.

Twenty-five years ago, Claire and I attended an international Catholic Worker gathering in Las Vegas that featured the head of the United Farm Workers, César Chávez, and Brazilian archbishop Dom Helder Camera, but, because I had laryngitis, I couldn't say a word all weekend.

No one remembers I was even there.

"And now," Karen croaked, "look what's happening to the weather."

Indeed, the forecast had deteriorated from sunny to partly cloudy to chance of showers all the way to outright rain, and we still have three days left for it to get worse. Light rain, something I call Irish dew, is okay, but downpours stink. I mean that quite literally. The last time I ran in cold rain, my nostrils felt like they were pressed up against a wet dog.

Beside olfactory annoyance, cold weather has increasingly triggered a condition called Raynaud's Syndrome. For reasons only those spiteful occupants of Mount Olympus can fathom, my fingers turn ghostly white and lose all sensation, as if they were frostbitten. It's some kind of incurable circulatory problem.

A visit to WebMD told me that a French doctor, Auguste Gabriel Maurice Raynaud, first identified the odious affliction in 1862. Primary Raynaud's is harmless, but the secondary version could be a sign of lupus or rheumatoid arthritis. Since those sound terrifying, I have resolved not to look them up. Apparently, one in ten people have some form of Raynaud's, but it's nine times more likely in women, in men or women with carpal tunnel syndrome, or in people who "use vibrating tools like jackhammers." What the flip? I'm male, don't have carpal tunnel, and have never even touched a jackhammer!

My annual physical is scheduled for July. The list of maladies trying to kill me gets longer all the time. I better tell my doctor to set aside an entire day for the exam. I'm preparing myself to say, "Give it to me straight, Doc. I can take it. How much time do I have left?" After all, what's the point of being a hypochondriac if I'm going to contract actual diseases?

On the sunny side, we don't have to bake this coming weekend, so I don't have to confront the lights-on, lights-off, spooky-noise-filled Phelan Center. Yippee!

As if my medically challenged, pre-marathon, hysterical self didn't have enough to worry about, something else sabotaged my peace of mind. The telephone at our house rings, on average, thirty times a day, mostly with calls from homeless people, social workers, family, friends, telemarketers, and women saying we have won a free Caribbean cruise, but, from time to time, we pick up the receiver and hear nothing. We say, "Hello?" a few times and hang up. Whether those calls are wrong numbers or evidence of government surveillance is unclear. For a time, Claire suspected a would-be burglar wanted to ascertain whether or not we were home, but since no one has burgled us, I think we can rule that out. Ever since we changed carriers last year, our phone has had Caller ID, an amenity I sure hope they don't charge us for. When we get those mysterious calls, unfamiliar numbers display on the screen. I suppose a real detective would dial them, but I have not bothered to do so. Frankly, given how needful most of our calls are, it's nice to get a few that require nothing from us at all.

What isn't nice are the type of voiceless calls that have been coming of late. As with the others, no one responds when I say, "Saint Francis and Thérèse Catholic Worker," but unlike previous calls, I get the distinct impression that someone lurks on the line. I hear breathing. The display always says *UNKNOWN CALLER*. While the experience differs only slightly from the usual nobody-there calls, it still unsettles me. I can't shake the feeling that the other party makes some kind of weird threat. Strangely, when I asked Claire and Aiden, they both said they hadn't received a single similar call when they answered the house phone. How could I be the only one getting them?

The next time I get a silent stalker call, I should resolutely challenge the culprit and say, "I am not afraid!" The trouble is, my voice would probably quaver unconvincingly like the protagonists' in Arnold Lobel's masterpiece *Frog and Toad Are Friends*[53]. When Arnold Schwarzenegger says, "Your clothes, give them to me," in *The Terminator*[54], a guy can't take his off fast enough, but I have no such vocal authority. Now, if I had James Earl Jones's voice of "Luke,-I-am-your-father[55]" and the Sprint Facebook commercial fame[56] or Yul Brynner's from

The Ten Commandments[57], I could say, "Bring me a doughnut" and be holding an assorted dozen in a nanosecond. As it is, Rodney Dangerfield got more respect than I ever will.

Nineteen years ago, I convinced my daughter, Grace, and sons, Patrick and Aiden, to appear in a play I called, *MacBeth: The Short Form.* Inspired by episodes of *The Little Rascals*[58] when Alfalfa interprets Romeo and Spanky eulogizes Caesar, I edited the Bard down to a six-scene production lasting fifteen minutes. With such a small cast, we had to make adjustments like having only two witches instead of three, but, otherwise, we stuck to the original, though shortened, script. In the climactic scene, three-year-old Aiden points a sword at MacBeth, aka Patrick, and says, "Turn, hellhound, turn!" I'm afraid, even Aiden had a delivery more convincing than anything I could muster.

Perhaps if I listen very closely, I will garner some clues. In crime dramas, police tape the kidnappers' calls and then scrutinize the recordings for the tiniest background noise in order to figure out where to apprehend the villains. Maybe if I take the receiver into the quietest room in our house, I might catch the kind of distinctive sound that yields an aha moment. A very specific foghorn, for example, might suggest that the culprit was skulking on the ferry to Block Island or Provincetown. Unfortunately, a criminal mastermind might pepper his or her calls with bogus effects to throw me off the trail. Darn it.

I called Karen for advice, got an answering machine, and had to settle on leaving a message.

"Good Grief!" I said. "What kind of a sidekick are you that doesn't even answer her phone?"

She called me later to confess that, when she played my message back, she couldn't understand a word I said.

I could not escape the fact that, when another spooky call comes in, I'm just going to have to wing it, as Barry Manilow[52] used to croon, "all by myself."

Friday, May 4

It's official. I'm either dealing with Evil or cracking up again.

After a million comfortable evenings, a mini-heat wave converted our house into an oven. In an effort to get the eight hours sleep Karen's marathon plan insists on, I climbed into bed at eight, cast off the blanket, spread, and sheets, and lay there sweltering. Claire, busy finishing an article she has been researching and writing for months, remained glued to her laptop. After reading a few pages in *Magpie Murders*[59], an Anthony Horowitz mystery my daughter Grace highly recommended, I drifted off into the arms of Morpheus.

Not long after I turned fifty, I started waking up at night with a need to pee, an apparently normal circumstance for older men. Since I refused medication for it, my doctor suggested that I restrict my fluid intake after dinner, but I've always resisted following his or any other medical professional's advice, so I get up to pee. Thankfully, I have no trouble getting back to sleep after relieving myself. And yet, especially when I have to rise three or four times a night, I suspect the phenomenon may account for disturbing my mental health. Perhaps it explains why I forgot my pants. Who knows?

At any rate, last night, I made my first foray to the toilet at 10:35 while Claire continued to work away. I woke again when she came to bed at midnight and yet again around 2. By that time, with Claire beside me, I felt wicked hot. After making the trip to pee yet another time, I flopped from front to back in a vain campaign to deter sweat. Finally, I drifted to sleep on my side facing Claire. She snores a tiny bit, something I keep saying I am going to tape record for posterity but haven't gotten around to yet.

Just as I started to cross the threshold to dreamland, I felt a tap on my back. Since my side of the bed faces the door, I turned to see if Aiden or one of our guests had come downstairs, but I saw no one there. Assuming the tap had been part of a dream, I lay on my stomach with my arms outstretched and face buried in my pillow (Not to be confused with the internet sensation Mypillow[60]). Because our bed isn't that big and Claire hogs most of it (another point of contention), my right arm draped off the side as I succumbed to the Sandman[61]. I must have been exhausted, because I rarely sleep on my stomach.

Before I could rev up the rapid eye movement, though, I felt an icy hand clasp my wrist and pull me almost off the bed. I yanked free and sat upright, instantly wide awake. I felt uncomfortably sure that the sensation did not constitute part of any dream. I could swing my head over the side and look under the bed to confirm whether or not anyone waited in ambush there.

Yah, right. Like I would ever do *that*.

Instead, I shook Claire, an action that provoked groggy disapproval. I turned on the light, squashing her as I reached over to do so. She slept on. Emboldened by the LED, I hopped out of and well clear of the bed and, from that safe distance, peeked underneath only to see nothing but dust bunnies.

This was not good. Seeing lights going on and off at their own will, hearing strange noises, and receiving mysterious phone calls might discombobulate me, but getting grabbed was much worse.

As Ian Michael Smith exclaimed in *Simon Birch*[62], I muttered, "Not happy. Not happy."

When I finally returned to bed, I lay with my back up against Claire as my eyes swept the perimeter back and forth for signs of a poltergeist. Although I determined to be vigilant, sleep must have overtaken me, because in what seemed like a minute, my alarm clock said, "Time to make the doughnuts."

I placed my feet on the throw rug by the bed, but no pale icy hands reached out to grab my ankles. Alleluia!

Now you may consider me silly at fifty-nine to worry about monsters under the bed, but I assure you that such fear isn't irrational. Claire's and my dear friend, Tom Lewis, cheerfully printed antiwar woodcuts in the afternoon and died from a heart attack that evening. Each and every one of us is going to die. That's a cold hard fact. In Anne Rice's novel, *Memnoch the Devil*[63], the protagonist hears Satan's footsteps approaching. The Squirrel Nut Zippers' incongruously cheerful song "Hell" has a verse advising:

> People listen attentively,
> I mean about future calamity.
> I used to think the idea was obsolete
> Until I heard the old man stamping his feet.

In bygone days, people believed a black-hooded spectre would foretell their deaths. An episode of *The Twilight Zone* called "One for the Angels" casts Murray Hamilton, mayor of Amity in *Jaws*[64], as an Angel of Death clad in a plaid suit.

The attire doesn't really matter. In most accounts, no one but the doomed individual can see his or her executioner. If that's actually true, then why can't a harbinger of death grab me from under the bed? While I'd prefer to receive notification by certified mail or not at all, I doubt rules or even protocols govern how the bad news gets delivered. Having seen my fair share of death, I don't care what Blue Öyster Cult[65] or anyone else sings about it. I will fear the reaper.

Sunday, May 6

A great day nearly spoiled.

Providence's weather was almost perfect for a marathon: cloudy, fifty-eight degrees with a slight cooling wind. Claire dropped me off at the luxurious Omni Hotel where I had to pick up my bib—not the kind infants don to keep their onesies clean, but the paper variety with a race number on the front and a computer chip on the back to record a runner's time. The chip verifies whether or not participants actually complete the full 26.2 miles. I heard about twins who cheated their way to victory by running only half a race each while sharing the same bib.

I bounded up the escalator to the second-floor ballroom and took out my driver's license. No one gets a bib without ID, a hurdle set up to prevent turtles from hiring rabbits to race in their stead. You'd be surprised how low some runners will stoop in order to record better times.

I was feeling mighty good until the fox in the henhouse sidled up beside me at the pickup table. It was the more-alive-than-dead Mr. Red Hand wearing an odious Boston Athletic Association shirt. (Although the BAA hosts one of the world's most iconic marathons and has a cool unicorn logo, the organization has a reputation for notorious greediness and stinginess. While most marathons end with a feast and free beer, when you cross the finish line in Boston, the BAA gives you a banana, bun, and bag of chips. I've long wanted to make a custom shirt with their logo proclaiming, "The BAA. We don't care. We don't have to.") Why would anyone wear that shirt?

"What the flip?" I thought. "He's a runner too? If so, he's the first dead one I've ever seen."

His appearance threw me off so much that I dropped my bib. By the time I retrieved it, he was heading for the lobby. Following at a safe distance, I bumped into my friends Jack Goolsky and his partner, Jenny McKenzie, there to run the half marathon that began a half hour after the marathon. I had told Jack the previous day at Worcester State that I was glad to hear they planned to run because I might need Jen's medical help.

"You know," he told me, "she's a urologist."

"Not a problem," I replied, "I've alienated so many doctors that, at this point, I'd take advice from a zoologist."

Jack and I are almost the same age, but he is a more experienced runner. I asked him if he could fix the settings on a Garmin watch so Karen could get reminded if she exceeded or lagged behind her goal pace. Jack worked his magic, and Karen appeared just after he and Jen moved on. By that point, I had lost sight of Red Hand. With more than twelve hundred runners, nothing guaranteed my seeing him again.

As the 7:30 start time approached, Karen and I joined the throng inside the barricades dividing us from spectators. As planned, we sought out a pacer holding aloft a sign reading "9 Minutes." That pace would bring us in at just under four hours. Karen had to beat four hours and I had to be five minutes faster to qualify for the 2019 Boston Marathon. Pacers are saints who run to help others reach their goals. Supposedly, six or seven additional pacers had faster and slower targets on their signs, but I didn't see them in the crowd.

After the national anthem (a proceeding that I wish had prompted me to take a knee in solidarity with Colin Kapernick[66] now that the NFL has made protesting against racism a mortal sin), a gunshot signified the start of the race. We shuffled along until we crossed the sensor mats so the computer could record us and started our respective watches. By the time we had gone a couple of blocks, we each had enough space to run comfortably, which we did with ease. We chatted together. I felt great, so much so that when Karen had to stop at a porta potty, I actually waited for her before resuming the race. Way back in February, when we trained at ten minutes a mile, Karen doubted she'd ever maintain a nine-minute pace, but our training had paid off. We felt so good that we passed the pacer and effortlessly crested the first hill. I wondered if I was finally running a marathon that wouldn't implode.

After three miles, though, I found myself ahead of Karen. I shouted at her, and she replied with a wave of her hand, "Don't wait for me. Go on." I eventually did while taking care not to go faster than 8:40.

Suddenly, at about the six-mile mark, as I ascended a rather long hill, Red Hand sped by. While everyone gets passed at some point during a 26.2-mile race, no one enjoys seeing someone do it with ease. I'm a pretty good hill runner, but he belonged to an entirely different class. With a light step, relaxed posture, and perfect form, he reminded me of an elite runner.

Given that he has at least thirty-five pounds on me, I almost blurted out, "How can a guy as fat as you run that fast?" a question I have actually asked other portly runners, as Karen will testify.

My high school cross-country coach taught us to run while imagining the ground as a hot frying pan we wanted to touch as briefly as possible. Too many runners slap their feet down as if squashing hard-shelled insects. When I hear them do it, I can well imagine shock waves reverberating up their legs. Most runners also slow way down on hills, and some even walk. Light on his feet and seemingly indefatigable, Red Hand didn't even appear to sweat. In short order, he ran far ahead of me.

Until that point, I hadn't decided how I felt about him. His contradictory affiliations, combative personality, and far-flung appearances confused me, but his athletic prowess clarified things. After seeing how well he runs, I knew I hated his guts.

Despite months of careful training to avoid another catastrophic marathon, the sight of him in the distance spurred me to run faster. By mile ten, I closed on him. Gone was my vow to keep my pace between 8:30 and 8:45 per mile. My Garmin screamed at me, "AHEAD OF PACE!" I didn't care. By mile twelve, I ran at 7:50. If it took a 7-minute mile to beat that super-athletic whale, I'd dig down deep to manage it.

As I approached, I heard him talking (can you believe it? I'm dying and he's talking) to two young women. Apparently, they had never run a marathon. As a man who likes to share wisdom with newbies, I could relate, but I did not hear anything of the kind from him. Drawing on impressive race credentials, he dispensed terrible advice.

"Your middle miles should be at a sprint pace," he said. And then, "Only take water every nine miles or you could get Hyponatremia, a potentially deadly condition. Also, clench your hands into fists to help power your arms."

Even though Hyponatremia is a real thing, you'd almost have to drown yourself before you can get it. A novice wouldn't know that, but I knew he was pedaling bullshit.

As we neared two long tables with volunteers holding out cups and saying, depending on which one they held, "Water" or "Gatorade," I hoped the women would ignore Red Hand, but they didn't. Worse still, when they turned away from him to reject the drinks, he smirked.

Realizing that he wanted to ruin their race (and, by association, mine, too), I slowed down. Had I not done so, I'm sure I would have had another breakdown. As it was, by mile 20, my body screamed, "What are you doing to me?"

Were it not for Claire leaving the sidelines and running beside me repeating, "One step at a time" and "You can do it" for the last two miles, I might have given up. However, with her encouragement, I ground it out finishing at 3:45 and change, almost ten minutes ahead of what I needed to qualify for Boston. It was my third best marathon.

I remained near the finish line until Karen also achieved her goal. At 3:58, she beat her record by more than two hours.

Although part of me wanted to seek out and confront Red Hand, Claire and I had to leave quickly in order to make an evening flight to Düsseldorf, Germany. To tell you the truth, the majority of me was eager to put an ocean between me and the birth-marked heat merchant[67].

Tuesday, May 8, 10:30 A.M.

I'm sitting in Saint Peter's Lutheran Church in Dortmund, a city in Germany's industrial heartland pulverized during World War II. As Claire and I saw in photos at the entrance, the barest shell of the reconstructed building had survived the bombardment.

Bernd Büscher and his wife, Sabine, are our charming hosts. Bernd picked us up at the airport, and then we shared a much-appreciated meal with Sabine and their friend Chris, a single mother of a fourteen-year-old son. Bernd and Sabine have two sons, one of whom played in a screamo band like Aiden used to. In an angry, raspy voice, Bernd mimicked his son singing, "Alleluia." Although screamo makes heavy metal seem light, Bernd confirmed what Aiden told us that many of its adherents don't drink, take drugs, or engage in pre-marital sex. Wild.

Bernd and Chris are part of the extended community that runs the Kana Catholic Worker Soup Kitchen, named in German for the location where Jesus turned water into wine. Both Protestants, they are nonetheless well-informed about the Catholic Worker movement. Bernd visited CW houses in Iowa and is close with our CW friends there, Brian Terell and Frank Cordaro. Bernd wrote to the New York Catholic Worker many times but didn't get a reply. He didn't realize that, unless he addressed his letters to a particular person, no one would answer. In contrast, the midwestern Catholic Worker communities immediately invited him to visit.

Bernd spent time in Iowa at the Des Moines CW house and Malloy CW Farm. He also stayed at the Rock Island,

Illinois, Catholic Worker house with Chuck Trapkus, one of the most talented and remarkable people I ever met. A gifted artist and artisan who railed against overuse of technology, Chuck died in a car accident, a strange twist of fate.

Our friend Frits ter Kuile of the Amsterdam Catholic Worker invited Claire and me to Germany. Every spring, Frits has tried to get us to come to European Catholic Worker gatherings, which take place in alternate years in Germany or England. He has visited the states for similar CW get-togethers in Las Vegas and Worcester. His community hosted Claire and our daughter Grace in 1999 when Claire attended the Hague Appeal for Peace alongside over nine thousand activists, government representatives, and community leaders from more than a hundred countries. Grace, who was almost eleven at the time, only recently told us that she and Amendine, a French-African girl she befriended at the Hague, started each day by scooping out change from a fountain and then using it to buy snacks as they explored the city.

When *Nothing Is Impossible* came out, Frits ordered a dozen copies, sent them to all the European Catholic Worker houses, and offered to set up speaking engagements for Claire and me. The prospect of selling books and a generous bequest to Saints Francis and Thérèse house in the will of Father Rocco Piccolomini convinced us to make the journey.

While we found it exotic to be in Germany, Saint Peter's Church is wicked sterile. To the left of the altar something that looks like a forty-foot-high pile of enormous wooden Jenga blocks covers organ pipes with the keyboard in front.

Bland windows, frosted off-white, rise to my left and right, with others behind the altar. Without the authentic stained glass Aiden restores at his job in Upton, Massachusetts, the church seems less sacred to me. It has no pews, just a circle of modern chairs around a golden cloth on the floor with four fat candles and a bronze incense holder. In a sign of how far ecumenism has gone, a Buddhist mindfulness bell sits on a small red cushion next to a wooden striker that looks like a seven-inch baseball bat.

Claire and I ended up in Saint Peter's Church in the center of Dortmund after Bernd guided us on the subway. We're speaking tonight at Kana and sightseeing beforehand. There are four old churches in the city center. We'll probably see them all. At London's Heathrow Airport, where Claire and I had a seven-hour layover, we alternately slept and walked around. In one of the shops, I saw the latest issue of *The Economist* magazine. Its cover title, "Marx was right about some things," appeared over a drawing of Communism's founder wearing a red baseball hat with the logo, "Make Socialism Great Again."

At the airport, I saw Harrod's, Gucci, and other very high-end stores I might otherwise never encounter. Claire and I had a wickedly overpriced lunch with super small portions and warm water that smelled skunky to me as we sat beside a huge ad for Rolex watches, including one for an eighteen-carat white gold version. The thing that struck me is that the wrist watch had a little knob for setting the time and, perhaps, winding. Call me crazy, but I don't think I'd pay a jillion dollars for a timepiece that looks like it's made of aluminum and that I still have to wind up.

Tuesday, May 8, 11 A.M.

We're now in Dortmund's Saint John the Baptist Catholic Church, only slightly less antiseptic than Saint Peter's due to a few abstract blue and white stained glass windows. Happily, though, a cozy, vaulted side chapel boasts an ornate dove-shaped monstrance behind its altar. Wooden pews in the main church and a smattering of medieval art diminish the feeling that the edifice is a poor substitute for what was destroyed by war.

A woman at a side altar fills a bottle with holy water. Carrying a huge purse and massive shopping bag, she wears yellow jeans and a shiny, leopard-skin top. She just removed a second bottle from her bag. And several more. She's actually filling five bottles!

Does she plan to battle Evil?

She crosses to the opposite side altar to drop coins in a box and light candles before a statue of Mary. A couple joins her to make a donation for votive candles. I think Protestants miss out on important fund-raising opportunities.

In a nearby pew, Claire writes in her journal. She tells me I cannot read it until ten years after her death. I tell her to underline my name to simplify things for me.

Tuesday, May 8, Noon

We're in the back of a Protestant church half filled with people singing in German with an organ accompanying them. I think it's Saint Mirjam's. A woman minister, all in black save a crossed white scarf in front, ascends a golden lectern shaped like an eagle. Once again, appallingly modern stained glass surrounds me as well as what appears to be more antique art, including an ornate medieval triptych bordered by two bouquets of balloons. Imitation candles festoon an ornate chandelier. I recognize about every seventh or eighth word the minister says. In German, each individual word stands out unlike in some languages where everything seems to squish together in an incomprehensible blur.

A pianist leads the congregation in joyful song. I feel a bit like an alien visiting earth for the first time as I wonder what the heck human beings are doing.

Tuesday, May 8, 12:30 P.M.

The last church of the day, this one dedicated to Saint Reinhold, the patron of Dortmund. A Benedictine monk and stonemason, he was beaten to death with hammers by other masons jealous of his skill. Although they had his body dumped in a pool near the Rhine, it miraculously returned to cause all the sick to be healed. In his church, the oldest in Dortmund, we finally discovered a couple of original pieces of stained glass in marvelous blues and reds. As nice as they are, though, the big kahuna in this church is an enormous statue of Saint Dortmund himself wielding a sword. He looks like a super hero.

We need a bathroom. Have you ever tried to find a public restroom in Manhattan? (My editor tells me there's a free one in Bryant Park and another free one in Trump Tower. Let's make New York great again.) Our quest felt daunting. The church has bathrooms that tantalized us through the windows of securely locked doors. An attendant suggested we'd find ladies' and men's rooms in an adjacent department store, so off we went.

It felt weird, after visiting four churches, to ride multiple escalators past clothing by Calvin Klein, Ralph Lauren, Tommy Hilfiger, and others I didn't recognize but know I can't afford. I prayed that I didn't look so bedraggled that some flunky would ask me to buy something or leave.

Since Claire got out on the third floor with my facilities reported on the fourth, I was on my own. It took me quite a while to find the bathroom tucked away in a corner with a sign that meant nothing to me. Unfortunately, the damned entrance has a modern turnstile beside a sleek payment machine. I had to cough up a Euro to pee. Luckily, I had the required coin, which looks to me like tokens you get at Scrubadub[68] and Chuck E. Cheese's[69]. Once I lowered the high tech drawbridge, I entered a bathroom so clean I feared I might go snow blind. Weirdest of all, after I turned to leave, I heard an automatic flushing sound followed by a humming noise. When I turned to see what that was about, I saw the seat of the toilet slowly rotating under some kind of sterilizer. The mechanism would erase all evidence of my visit. I regret I didn't have a magic marker so I could write a limerick on the wall.

When I descended to the first floor and emerged onto the promenade (I'm just assuming that's what they call the pedestrian-only area packed with stores, except they say it in German), the first person I saw was the most disheveled man I have ever seen, and I've seen quite a few. His clothes in tatters, his hair hanging limply around his dirty face, and his feet swollen, bleeding, and bare, he was unimaginably out of place in the ritzy surroundings. Moving glacially with downcast eyes, he didn't have to beg for help. His entire being appealed desperately for assistance.

I approached him, pressed Euros into his hand, and asked if I could help him in any way. He shook his head and moved on, almost like a ghost.

Tuesday, May 8, 10 P.M.

Claire and I just returned from an outdoor café with Bernd, Chris, and another member of the Kana Catholic Worker named Birke. What fantastic beer! Bernd told us that Dortmund reigned as Germany's beer capital until a conglomerate bought out local brewers and closed the plants. Thankfully, microbreweries sprang up to save the integrity of a German mainstay.

Ranging from politics to religious philosophy, conversation with our new German friends stimulated all of us. Bernd has a warm smile that lights up his face. Birke is smart and curious. Chris is frank and good humored. At the end of our time, she asked me, "How can you be so fucking optimistic?"

Earlier in the evening, we presented our talk in the remarkably tidy Kana soup kitchen where Catholic Workers serve up to two hundred lunches on weekdays. It went well. The crowd of about twenty-five people paid close attention to Claire, laughed at my stories, asked good questions, and bought a few books. What more could we ask for?

Unfortunately, a disconcerting thing occurred on our way back from church hopping. After a stop for Claire to get coffee, eat chocolate, and write in her journal while I stretched out to read *Magpie Murders*, we caught a train back to Bernd and Sabine's lovely home. I sat facing a father and son. The young boy had Harry Potter eye glasses, wore an Incredible Hulk T-shirt, and sucked on a lollipop while clutching a Paw Patrol bag. His dad's black shirt proclaimed, "Sex, drugs, and rock n' roll." To my right, several teens joked with each other. Although they spoke a foreign language, the scene struck me as universal.

When the slightly swaying cars slowed down at a station, I asked Claire, "Is this our stop?" She's a wiz at navigating subways, while I have an unmatched sense of direction above ground. Where would we be without each other?

After she said, "One more," I looked out onto the platform and saw Red Hand!

Fitted out this time in a tailored suit and tie, he strode confidently by with his birth-marked hand holding a briefcase at his side. He looked straight forward, moved with purpose, and never glanced in my direction. Yet, I had the uncanny feeling he knew I recognized him and that his innocuous walk actually served as an insidious parade for my benefit alone.

Seeing him in Worcester, Westborough, and Providence was unlikely yet possible, but seeing him thousands of miles away from New England shocked me. Was he following me? And, if so, why?

Truth be told, he didn't stand out in the crowd among other businessmen. Had he sported paraphernalia for the right-wing, anti-immigrant Alternative for Germany Party or, worse still, neo-Nazis, I would have drawn Claire's attention to him, but, save the birth-mark, he appeared unexceptional. He didn't look like a vampire, ghoul, zombie, or ghost. And he didn't pick a fight with anyone either. For all I knew, he could have been on the way to a meeting, but, somehow, I doubted that. My men's intuition told me he was up to no good.

Wednesday, May 9

We are now in Dülmen, an absolutely gorgeous place by a small lake about an hour and a half's drive from Dortmund. We rose early, and I ran five miles on a heavily used bike trail through Bernd's neighborhood. Then Frank, one of the Kana Catholic Workers we met last night, drove us here. Nestled in woods surrounded by farms, the Dülmen Catholic Workers gather at a camp by a lake where I took a refreshing swim. Birke and her daughter Leah went in as well. Margrite, from Holland, joined us. I could see swans in the distance. Claire and I have a cozy room with bunk beds in one of three buildings that make up the camp.

I'm sitting in a central meeting space off our room and five others. Through large plate glass windows and glass doors to my left, I can see rhododendrons in full bloom, some with purple flowers like those in our yard back home but others with brilliant red ones. Beyond a few bushes and trees lies the lake. Through windows to my right, I can see a small soccer field with pastures in the distance. I'm told this is the only part of Germany with wild horses.

Frank told us the organizers expect about fifty people, a bigger crowd than I imagined. Boxes of food we helped carry in from Bernd's van look delicious. Fresh strawberries, blueberries, peaches, tangerines, yogurt, and much more. I'm told there's a bonfire every night.

I didn't imagine our trip as a vacation, but it certainly seems like one right now. Claire is out running and plans to swim when she returns. As people arrive, I write their names phonetically with a description that I hope will help me identify them later on.

First there's Uta from the Brot und Rosen (Bread and Roses) Catholic Worker in Hamburg. She has short hair, a green shirt, and yellow pants. Second, there's Birgit, also from Hamburg. She wears a necklace with a carved elephant and then, Dietrich, Uta's husband, in a Papua New Guinea T-shirt; two young women from the Amsterdam CW, Sophie with long hair and Indian pants, and Margrite, with a broad smile and wide eyes. Tareah, a slightly older woman in a green hat, is also from Holland. A young blond Dutchman in glasses is Harm-Jan. Lodzt, a heavy-set, completely bald Jesuit priest from the Catholic Worker in Essen came with a bearded Jesuit named Lutegar.

My notes continue. Clare is a cheerful American with a great singing voice: she spent time at the Los Angeles, London, and Calais Catholic Worker houses. Veronika is a tall blond German with sad eyes, a kind smile, and prominent cheeks. Short with brown hair in a pony tail, Alma is trying to start a community in northern Sweden. Daan is a short, well-educated, good-humored young man from the Amsterdam house. Nora, a woman with long black hair and friendly disposition, is a German-born member of Giuseppe Conlon Catholic Worker in London. Richard is a lanky, quite spiritual man who once struggled with alcohol and spent some time on the streets before helping to found the Dover, England, Catholic Worker. Mirjam is a short, blond Swede, with a marvelous voice and also part of the London CW. Herman, his wife Anna, and their newborn baby, Naomi, are from Amsterdam, or as my granddaughter May calls it, Hamsterdam.

I meet more people. (I'm going to need a personal secretary to sort them out.) Martin, a Passionist priest, helped start the London house as well as one where he resides in Birmingham. He has the distinction of being one of the few English speakers Germans have trouble understanding. Frits is a ball of energy and joy out of Amsterdam, as is Susan, whom Claire and I knew from her participation in a past nuclear disarmament protest. Clive, a wonderful salt-and-pepper-bearded man, founded the Oxford, England, Catholic Worker and hosted Claire and me along with our children for two days during our 1996 journey to India. Several more teens and another family as well as a few more individuals completed the roster, including Irmtraud, an older German from Italy who is passionate about the need to enact universal basic income and a rail-thin, long haired German who reminded me of many old-time radicals. If each person had only worn the same clothes for three days, I could have learned their names without checking my notebook, but, alas, they did not.

After a delicious meal served on long tables in a building with a large meeting room off a kitchen, everyone shared community updates. The Europeans impressed Claire and me with their ability to serve the needy without giving up peace and justice work, a commitment to prayer, or their personal and family lives.

In a clearing not far from our sleeping quarters, benches and seats surrounded a fire. From ten until the wee hours of the morning, folks sat, talked, joked, sang songs, drank beer or wine, toasted marshmallows, and ate chocolate. After reading

The Brothers Karamazov[70] a third time, Daan told me he
finally understands why Dorothy Day loved it so much.

"Every character is a bit of divine revelation," he said.

When I was an undergrad at Holy Cross College, my
friends and I had similarly lofty conversations. It's one thing
to have such discussions without experience of poverty, injustice, war, and life in community. It's another thing to actually
try, as the Catholic Worker cofounder Peter Maurin urged,
"to make a world where it's easier to be good." No one said
anything phony, trite, or pretentious around that fire. Folks
who live and work with the poor identify with Dostoevsky's
proclamation, "Love in dreams is easy, but love in action is
a harsh and dreadful thing." And yet, the fact that Catholic
Workers are not at all morose drew me to the movement.
In fact, virtually all CWs have generous senses of humor.
Although I had known most of those Europeans for less than
a day, our similar outlook toward life created an instantaneous
camaraderie. In a world of so much isolation, insecurity, and
self-consciousness, the Catholic Worker movement validates
the best in each one of us.

When I finally peeled off to go to sleep, I felt so refreshed
that even another sighting of Red Hand would not have
disconcerted me.

Thursday, May 10

Claire rose early to join Richard and others for twenty minutes of meditation around the still smoldering fire. Meanwhile, I helped Alma arrange chairs in a circle for morning prayer in the meeting space just outside Claire and my bedroom. About twenty people, including the meditators, joined us. The prayer opened with Taizé chant from the popular interfaith monastery in France where, thirty-nine years earlier, Claire spent a transformative two days. Thanks to Will Raymond, a musician who's a regular at our bimonthly evening prayer in Worcester, Claire and I know many of those chants. Besides singing, the prayer included a psalm, Gospel reading, petitions, The Lord's Prayer, and a considerable period of silence.

As a novice with the Capuchin-Franciscans from 1980 to 1981, I was expected to meditate for thirty minutes each morning before Mass but must confess that, in order to keep myself from falling asleep, I concentrated my attention on reliving a childhood visit to Disneyland. While other novices tried to make space for the Holy Spirit, I strolled through the gates of the enchanted castle, climbed the Swiss Family Robinson tree house, and enjoyed the Pirates of the Caribbean ride. When Brother Jerry Rocco, who sat next to me in chapel, asked how I could sit so prayerfully still, I didn't have the courage to answer him.

Two years later at Saint Benedict's Catholic Worker in Washington, DC, I made a more serious stab at meditation. During the lead-up to daily Mass, I'd close my eyes, slow my breathing, and try to empty my mind. Oftentimes, I'd find myself in a black void where Jesus would appear. Unlike in the movies, a heavenly choir did not accompany Christ. He just showed up in a kind of spotlight, usually without saying a word or even looking at me, although one time I did see him wink. He struck me as an intriguing person.

Unfortunately, when I first shared my experience with Claire and our co-worker Carl Siciliano, they expressed skepticism, and, later, when I told them I had seen Jesus on a skateboard, they concluded I was a nut rather than a mystic. So, I gave up the practice.

On a whim, surrounded by amicable European Catholic Workers, I decided to give meditation another go. Since I was pretty rusty, it took considerable effort to clear my mind, and, even then, I only got to the void's doorstep, an inky wall without visible extremities. I got within inches of it and said, "Hello," which caused the surface to waver. Next, I poked it with my index finger. Since the digit appeared to be unharmed, I stuck my entire arm into the gravity-defying liquid. The other side felt neither hot nor cold. I wiggled my fingers easily and found no sign of discoloration when I withdrew them. Part of me wanted to stick my head in, but most of me felt apprehensive, so I contented myself with playing a silent hokey pokey (stick your right foot in, pull your right foot out, and you move it all about . . .) until Alma rang the mindfulness bell signaling the end.

Immediately after prayer, Claire, Margrite, Richard, Don, and I went running on a course Claire discovered the day before. Taking us past a farm onto a long tree-lined lane, the route was beautiful and mercifully flat. Richard and I drifted ahead of the others. To my chagrin, I learned he's an ultra athlete who trains daily with runs up and down the white cliffs of Dover. Now I know what Karen felt like. By its end, our pleasant morning jog had escalated into a 7:20 per mile race.

Once Claire and I returned to camp, we enjoyed a full day of talks, including two we gave, culminating in another fire circle. When I left the brightly lit, dining/meeting room to join the group, however, the night proved so dark that I had to stop on the path. Clouds obscured the stars, and the fire burned too far off to be of assistance. They say it takes your eyes ten minutes to fully adjust to darkness, so, rather than fall flat on my face on an unseen root or rock, I waited. While I did, the wind picked up and the air became quite cold. Instead of diminishing, the darkness seemed to deepen. An impression built that my birth-marked nemesis had tracked me down, but before I could either flee or fight, two German teens, using their cell phones as flashlights, rescued me.

Although I was only moderately shaken, I took no chances and slept with a nightlight.

Friday, May 11

Only seconds into today's meditation, I once again faced the dark wall but this time stuck my head right in followed by the rest of my body. Inky with no sense of up or down, the void nevertheless contained something that seemed able to support my feet. As a precaution, I reached behind me to confirm that I could escape if necessary. Having done so, I resolved to explore a bit.

Tentative steps gradually evolved into a relaxed stroll. On a whim, I leaned forward and realized I could move through the inky medium like a swimmer, astronaut, or bird. As a kid, I never mastered the somersault but easily completed one, settling quite naturally on the soles of my feet as if this were my thousandth rather than first tumble. In that environment, I felt unlimited potential without any fear. When a spark flared in the distance, I approached and discovered a tea light that I placed in the palm of my hand. As I continued walking, its illumination grew until I could make out vague shapes that slowly defined themselves into the trees and flowers overlooking the lake. With the bright sun warming my face, I realized I had been here the entire time, and, if I wanted to, could somersault and, if I desired, even fly.

Trust me. No way would I share that experience with Claire. She'd put me in the booby hatch before noon.

As it was, Lodzt and Lutegar drove Claire and me into the heart of Münster, a medieval college town hosting an annual event called the *Katholikentag* or Catholic Day even though the observance stretches over the entire weekend. Drawing thousands of people, *Katholikentag* features talks, concerts, art exhibits, and prayers in churches and on stages set up all over the old city. This year's theme, Suche Frieden or Seek Peace, proclaims itself on billboards citing Gandhi, Martin Luther King Jr., Rutilio Grande, Mother Theresa, and Oscar Romero. Bernd arranged for us to speak on Saturday, but suggested we spend some time today as tourists.

With map in hand, we wandered into a lovely square outside the Kiepenkerl pub where, on April 7, a man plowed his camper van through a crowd of people, injuring thirty and killing three. At first people suspected he might be an Islamic extremist, but it turned out he was mentally unstable with no terrorist affiliation. In the center of the square, a paschal candle leaned against the base of a statue depicting a medieval minstrel.

Bernd, Chris, and Birke shared with us how Germany had swung from enthusiastic welcome for refugees to divided public opinion with nationalists calling for severe reductions if not outright prohibition on new arrivals. All European Catholic Worker communities assist immigrants. Governmental social welfare services for citizens function far better than those in the United States, but, like in the US, immigrants, refugees, and people without documents struggle. As I saw on the promenade in Dortmund, no matter how extensive the safety net, some people still fall through the cracks.

The eight-hundred-year-old Catholic Cathedral of Saint Paul, like the churches in Dortmund, was devastated and then rebuilt after World War II. It contains the tomb of the former Bishop of Münster, Clemens August Graf von Galen, who became a cardinal shortly before his death in 1946. Pope Benedict XVI beatified him in 2005. Revered as one of the few members of the Catholic hierarchy who directly opposed the Nazis, von Galen condemned the Nazi worship of race in 1934. He helped draft Pope Pius XI's 1937 anti-Nazi encyclical *Mit Brennender Sorge* (*With Burning Concern*)[71]. In 1941, von Galen delivered three anti-Nazi homilies, including one that helped reverse the state-approved killing of invalids. Unfortunately, the Nazis sent those who published his sermons to concentration camps, while they left von Galen alone as a member of the German aristocracy.

Sad to say, von Galen never publicly opposed the rounding up and extermination of Jews. He was also an anti-communist whose writings were quoted by the Nazis in their attempt to recruit Dutchmen into the SS. Archbishop von Galen's apologists say he believed opposition to anti-Semitism would have provoked increased persecution of Jews and Catholics. In hindsight, it's hard to imagine anything worse than the Holocaust.

In contrast, a group of university students from Munich, led by Hans and Sophie Scholl, formed a resistance group called The White Rose in 1943. In their first of five leaflets, they wrote:

Nothing is more shameful to a civilized nation than to allow itself to be "governed" by an irresponsible clique of sovereigns who have given themselves over to dark urges – and that without resisting. Isn't it true that every honest German is ashamed of his government those days? Who among us can imagine the degree of shame that will come upon us and upon our children when the veil falls from our faces and the awful crimes that infinitely exceed any human measure are exposed to the light of day?

While von Galen survived, the Nazis arrested and executed members of The White Rose who remain shining lights of courage. I cannot strongly enough recommend the 2005 film *Sophie Scholl: The Final Days*, about The White Rose.

On the bright side, in the entrance to the cathedral, Claire and I found a stone from the Anglican cathedral in Coventry, England, destroyed by Germany on November 14, 1940. The stone was affixed under the heading "Deo Adjuante Resurgo" or "God helps us arise" and proclaims "Forgiving one another as God in Christ forgave you."

To the right of the memorial to reconciliation stands a bulletin board with a poster depicting Jesus snapping a gun in half over his knee and another that shows a Lego Jesus leading twelve Lego apostles. The headline reads, "Die Welt der kleinen Steine: ein Ostergarten aus Legosteinen," which means, "The World of Small Stones: an Easter garden made of Lego blocks." Sad to say, we didn't get to see that unique work of art.

Later, outside the six-hundred-year-old Saint Lambert's Church, Claire realized she has forgotten her cell phone in the crowded cathedral. Twenty minutes later, she joyfully rejoined me to say that a kind volunteer and a fortuitous run-in with Lutegar had reunited her with the device. Although I generally abhor cell phones, I would have been sad to see her lose all the photos she had taken with it.

After vain searches by Claire for chocolate and me for pretzels, we wound our way down a lovely wooded bike and pedestrian path to a church hosting a talk by international human rights activists. Since the speeches were not translated, I sat outside at a table to read, where I was surprised to find copies of the *German Catholic Worker* newspaper. A few minutes later, Frits, Chris, and others appeared carrying stacks of additional copies they planned to distribute on the street. Like early Catholic Workers in New York's Union Square, those Europeans overflowed with zeal, but since I couldn't say more than a dozen words in German, I stayed behind with the *Magpie Murders* novel Grace wanted me to finish before I returned home.

While engrossed in Anthony Horowitz's clever writing, I paid no attention to my surroundings. When Chris called out my name, however, I noticed a man getting up to leave two tables away from. It was Red Hand! Worse, he picked up a copy of the *German Catholic Worker*, dropped it in the trash, looked me right in the eyes, sneered, and sauntered away.

I had no idea how long he had sat nearby and shuddered to think about it. While he remained a mystery, his appearance made it crystal clear that he was following me.

Why? I'm not sure I wanted to know.

Saturday, May 12

Claire and I returned to Münster today with Bernd for our talk. I had no idea what to expect but was surprised to learn we would share the venue with a woman from Nonviolent Peaceforce. Since the organizers allotted only an hour and a half, I felt concerned but somewhat reassured because she promised to speak no longer than twenty minutes. As it happened, her presentation took fifty minutes during which I fretted that we'd come across the Atlantic to offer only a sound bite. But, lo and behold, my panic was uncalled for. Claire's brief remarks inspired me to speak concisely from my heart. Questions and comments, simultaneously translated for us via headphones, confirmed that our message resonated with the small audience. Even the translators said how much they enjoyed the talks. And most importantly, for my aching back, audience members purchased a few more books.

Afterwards, our host from one of the colleges and a friend of his invited us to coffee, something Claire drinks for both of us. We found them special people from whom we learned a great deal. With World War II having ended seventy-three years ago, I didn't expect to meet so many people still conscientiously struggling to learn from it. Sad to say, less than three decades after the Vietnam War, Americans got suckered into endless warfare in the Middle East. As Jorge Agustín Nicolás Ruiz de Santayana y Borrás, whom Americans call George Santayana, said so well, "Those who cannot remember the past are condemned to repeat it."

On our walk back to the train station with Bernd, he pointed out empty iron cages just below Saint Lambert's spire where Catholics exhibited bodies of tortured and then

Saint Lambert's Cages

executed leaders of an Anabaptist rebellion in 1536. Replicas of the original cages hang as reminders of religious intolerance. In July 2010, Catholics and Lutherans apologized for supporting persecution of Anabaptists during the Reformation. Interestingly, the brief Anabaptist reign in Münster reinforced the conviction of other Anabaptists to reject any use of violence and to preach love of the enemy. Calling themselves Mennonites after the sixteenth-century Dutchman Menno Simos who formalized early Anabaptist writing, they remain pacifists to this day.

When we arrived earlier in the morning, we carried many books and more than a thousand copies of the *German Catholic Worker*. Frits had distributed a few dozen copies the day before, but evidently no one else handed many out. Bernd managed to pass out several as we walked toward our train, but I decided instead to place them in the empty baskets of the bicycles parked everywhere. Apparently, Münster is known as a city of bicycles.

God rewarded me for my efforts too. In the entrance to the station, I thrilled to find heavenly soft pretzels for only one and half euros.

Back at the camp, everyone assured us we were in for a treat. Each European CW gathering includes a talent show as do many American gatherings. In the states, audiences tend to be very forgiving of the uneven, so-called talent. I expected as much in Germany but was pleasantly surprised. Impressive singing preceded a hysterical play about a hunt for a glow-in-the-dark statue of the Virgin Mary. Martin, acting as lead investigator, concluded each of his interrogations with, "Very suspicious. We'll be keeping an eye on you."

Teens held up signs saying "APPLAUSE" or urging us to echo Martin's "Very suspicious." Clive and Birke masterfully played Dorothy Day and Peter Maurin, the Catholic Worker cofounders. Nora gave a wonderful rendition of the song, "I Want to be Evil," which she personalized to include temptations all activists share.

But the highlight was a play written in English that very day by Daan. I recorded it on my spiffy little camera and transcribe it for you here.

Daan: Dorothy Day read *The Brothers Karamazov* over and over again on dark winter days. It gave her life. It gave her hope. But there is an interesting chapter in this book about a grand inquisitor. It's a story about Christ coming back in the sixteenth century, coming down to earth in the dark ages to the powerful Roman Catholic Church.

And the Roman Catholic Church is not amused by Christ coming back to earth. The Grand Inquisitor asks him some questions and tells Christ, "You shouldn't have come back here. We have taken over your business."

Dorothy Day probably didn't know what would be the effect of this Dostoevsky novel much later in the Catholic Worker movement.

So behold, see, and hear. Tremble. This is *The Short Loneliness*.

[For those who don't know, Dorothy Day's autobiography is entitled, *The Long Loneliness*[72].]

Sophie emerges from the kitchen door at stage left carrying a copy of The Brothers Karamazov *and plops down into a chair behind a table*

Sophie: Finally, some time on my own.

She leans back and opens the book.

Let's read Dostoevsky. Where was I? Ah, the Grand Inquisitor.

A knock at the door causes her to put down the novel and rise.

Sophie: Yah?

Harm-Jan enters.

Harm-Jan: Sophie, Sophie, I hope you're not too busy because . . .

Sophie: Well?

Harm-Jan: I really wanted to cook tonight and for the cooking I need . . .

Sophie: Money. Yah, yah.

She turns to get some.

Harm-Jan: . . . to get the groceries. So, can you give me some money?

She puts some money in his hand.

Sophie: Here. Okay, bye.

He looks down on what she's given him.

Harm-Jan: The last time I had only this much, but I really want to cook organic. It's a bit more expensive, so could you?

Sophie *(with two thumbs up)*: Yah, we're working on that.

Harm-Jan: We should really have a good discussion about that.

Sophie *(as she ushers him out)*: Yah, we should. Okay.

She closes the door, sits down again, and reopens the book.

Sophie: Finally, some time on my own. Where was I? The Grand Inquisitor.

More knocking at the door, causes her to sigh and put the book down. She gets up.

Sophie: Yah? Come in.

Herman enters.

Herman: Hey, you know your sign says "Do not disturb"?

Sophie: I know.

Herman: The fair-trade blue-tooth waffles have run out.

Sophie: Again?

Herman: Yah. Could you get some from the food pantry?

Sophie: I just bought them.

Herman: Yah. They were going fast, those waffles. Okay, bye.

He leaves. Sophie checks the other side of the door to see that her "Do not disturb" sign remains there. She closes the door, sits down, and takes up the book.

Sophie: Finally, some rest. I find it so difficult to get some time on my own!

Another knock on the door. Sophie slaps her book down on the table. Susan enters carrying a cell phone.

Susan: Sophie, hi. I've got a phone call here. It's really difficult, would you . . . ?

Sophie shakes her head "No" and gestures with her hands, but Susan holds it out to her.

Susan: I don't know. Here.

She places the phone in Sophie's hand and leaves. Sophie takes it up reluctantly. She speaks into the phone.

Sophie: Hi. This is the Catholic Worker. I'm Sophie.

Susan *(in a high-pitched voice off stage):* Hello, Sophie. I found your newsletter in the back of my church saying you give hospitality to people.

Sophie: Yah.

Susan: There're some people here—a mother and six children. And she's drunk, I think.

Sophie: Really sad. I wish you a lot of luck with that.

Susan: We donate every week. Surely you have a room.

Sophie: Actually, we don't have space at the moment. We're really full. All those people coming in.

Susan: You have to take them! I have to go to the cinema tonight.

Sophie *(exasperated)*: Okay, okay. Let them come. Bye.

She hangs us and picks up her book.

Sophie: Finally, some time on my own.

Another knock. Magrite enters.

Magrite: Sorry to disturb you. I know you're super busy.

Sophie: I am.

Margrite: You know Clare is arriving today?

Sophie: Wasn't she coming next week?

Magrite: No. Today.

Sophie: Oh.

Magrite: In the guest room there's a mother who seems to be drunk. She can stay in your room, right? She's drunk and musical.

In comes a smiling Clare, playing the ukulele. Magrite leaves.

Clare: I've got a new song. Do you want to hear it?

Sophie retrieves and opens her book.

Clare *(singing)*: The wheels on the bus go 'round and 'round . . .

Sophie puts her fingers in her ears. Another knock on the door. Frits enters carrying four crates.

Frits: A guy dropped those off, and there's more in his car. I've really got to go to the vigil. They're steaming vegetables. Can you take care of them? Thank you.

He puts them down, shakes her hand with both of his and backs out.

Frits: And there's more in the car.

Sophie bends over the crates and waves her hand in front of her nose while Clare sings. Sophie screams, pulls her hair, and sits down. She ignores another knock on the door. Clare continues to play the guitar.

Clare: I think there's someone at the door.

Herman enters carrying his newborn baby, Naomi.

Herman: You know, Michael brought donations. Some steaming vegetables. And some crates of frozen oysters back there. And at the bottom of this box, we found this thing, and I thought because you are going to be in your room for a while, so . . .

He places the baby in her arms and leaves. Sophie stands, bouncing the baby. Clare keeps singing. Sophie looks up at the ceiling.

Sophie: I wish I lived in a nuclear bunker with a lot of security where nobody could ever come.

Frits burst in, jumping up and down. He carries a large axe.

Frits: A nuclear bunker? Where is it? Let's go there and break it up.

Sophie: Actually, I just want to read my book by Dostoevsky.

Frits looks at the book.

Frits: Ah, yes. It's about war and peace, right? But tomorrow we'll go to this bunker, alright?

Sophie: Yah.

Frits pats her on the shoulder.

Frits: You enjoy the book.

Clare: The people on the bus go blah, blah, blah . . . "

Sophie: Clare, the dinner is almost ready. I will skip dinner because I need some rest today. I'll just stay in my room.

Clare: Okay.

The dinner bell rings. Clare gets up to leave, but Susan comes in carrying a pot and serving spoon.

Susan: Hi, Sophie. The dining room is taken. We are going to eat here.

Others stream in carrying plates and more pots. Chaos ensues until another knock on the door accompanied by the sound of celestial music. In comes Susan's mother, dressed like Dorothy Day with her hands folded in front of her as if in prayer. Daan goes over and kneels down in front of her and circles her.

Daan *(angrily)*: Is it thou? Is it thou? Don't answer! I already know thy answer. Thou doesn't have the right to come back and add anything to what I've written down in the third edition of *The Catholic Worker*. Right now, we take over your ideas. You didn't want to be a saint. You didn't want to be called saint. Well we decide who's a saint and not. And you are definitely a saint. (He points his finger.) And saints don't ring at the door when we are eating!! So, what the hell are you doing here? No, Mrs. Day, your time is over. Love in action is a harsh and dreadful thing.

He turns to the audience with raised arms.

Daan *(shouting)*: Can I get an "Amen?!"

After the crowd responds, he turns to "Dorothy Day."

Daan: And you knew it! So, why did you come with all those impossible ideas? Christian Anarchism! What a terrible idea! Don't you see we are desperate? *He pauses.* I want to ask two of my fellow workers to kick this woman out. *They escort her by her arms out the door.*

Seconds later, everyone returns, including Dorothy Day, and they dance to Clare's ukulele as they sing cheerfully.

Everyone (*to the tune of The Wheels on the Bus*):
Love in action is a harsh and dreadful thing,
dreadful thing, dreadful thing.
Love in action is a harsh and dreadful thing,
compared to love in dreams.

Anyone who has tried to work from home, especially a parent, can relate to Sophie's frustration. No sooner do you get settled in to work or take a break, and the phone rings or a child demands your attention. Those who live and work in communities dedicated to human service not only suffer interruptions but also feel guilty if they don't respond to them charitably.

On countless occasions, I cannot get even a single spoonful of lunch into my mouth before the doorbell or phone rings. For most Catholic Workers, I'd call it an occupational hazard, but in my case, it may be karma. Oftentimes, I make prank phone calls to Catholic Worker houses to test their Christian charity. Kathy Boylan often answers at Dorothy Day house in Washington, DC. She's my personal favorite. A typical call might run like this:

Kathy: Dorothy Day Catholic Worker. May I help you?

Me: Hello. I am the ambassador of the Colombian Embassy, and I am seeking shelter for a family of traumatized Venezuelan refugees who have been sleeping in their car. The five children have lice, and the parents have bed bugs. When he's sober, the father's English is good, although he prefers to use an obscure native dialect. When can I drop them off?

Kathy: Oh, dear. We'd love to help, but our house is very full right now.

Me: I've heard such wonderful things about your community. I was told you never turn anyone away. And, how could you? After all, the father's name is Jesus. I'll leave them at your door tonight at eleven.

And then I hang up.

A sweet person, Kathy represents low-hanging fruit for a prankster. She once believed I was an FBI agent named Bob Watkins.

She's not alone though. A volunteer at Maryhouse in New York City didn't blink when I identified myself as Pope Francis.

So you can imagine how much I enjoyed Daan's play, all the more so because it affirmed that the Catholic Worker sense of humor prevails in every country where people attempt to follow its ideals.

Sunday, May 13

Claire and I are comfortably settled in a second-floor room with bay windows in London's Giuseppe Conlon Catholic Worker house. In a rented van, Martin drove Clive, Richard, Mirjam, Nora, Claire, and me from Münster to Calais, France, where our vehicle was loaded onto a train to travel fifty-five kilometers through the Chunnel, the tunnel beneath the English Channel.

Heavily armed French troops ominously patrolled razor-wire topped barriers preceding the tunnel. Despite the perfunctory check soldiers gave our vehicle, I felt sick to my stomach imagining how terrifying that same scrutiny would be for families fleeing poverty and endless wars in Syria, Yemen, Afghanistan, Iraq, and sub-Saharan Africa. Would those soldiers really shoot families? According to Susan, who spent time at the Calais Catholic Worker where militarized police destroyed a huge camp of migrants, soldiers already have done so and are ready to do it again.

On the day before, Martin led a powerful workshop in Dülmen about the urgent need to confront what he called "the global emergency of climate change." Without belaboring the point, he made the case that humanity no longer has the luxury of incremental change. He said that people can ameliorate catastrophic environmental harm—already driving species to extinction and causing mass migration—but only by the kind of national commitments typically employed during wartime.

Humanity hurtles toward a precipice when carbon reduction takes a back seat to economic development, national security, and even leisure activities like tourism. And so

Martin argued that activists against war and poverty and for the environment have to unite in campaigns of civil disobedience to keep global warming on the front burner, so to speak. Primarily responsible for the crisis, wealthy nations have the greatest duty to act. None of us can claim innocence.

Martin recognized we must act simultaneously in shocking and hopeful ways lest we stoke fatalistic apathy. None of us can give up on the future, especially not folks like Claire and me with children and grandchildren.

During our flight from London to Düsseldorf, Claire and I marveled at how many large wind farms we saw at the mouth of the Thames, in the Channel, along the French and Dutch coast, and throughout the German countryside. In contrast, Worcester, a very windy city, has only one turbine. A project to build turbines off the shore of Massachusetts, first proposed in 2000 and vigorously opposed by wealthy residents of Martha's Vineyard, received final approval only this month with completion not expected until 2021.

Exponential growth of solar power transformed Massachusetts into a national leader. Virtually all of Worcester's public schools and many homes went solar, but reduced government incentives and sops to the oil and gas industries have slowed progress. Private and public investors continue to waste billions of dollars on new infrastructure for fossil fuels. With the state's last remaining nuclear power plant scheduled to go off line next year coupled with a failed deal to buy hydroelectric power from Canada, climate change skeptics insist we need to increase rather than decrease the use of natural gas, oil, and even coal. I believe the 1991 antiwar mantra, "No blood for oil," needs to be replaced with "No oil, period.

Martin insists that the world can technologically achieve a green energy revolution in as few as five years if as little as three percent of the population takes to the street to insist on it. To achieve the goal requires nothing short of total commitment similar to what the United States and its allies made to win World War II. That commitment totally transformed economies, and we can kick the carbon habit and become a green planet by dedicating ourselves similarly once again.

"With our activist creativity and the backing of Pope Francis's encyclical *Laudato Si*," Martin said, "Catholic Workers must be catalysts for environmental revolution."

While I listened to him, an idea began forming in my brain (as is said in *Time Bandits*[73]) that we might gather a group in Worcester for an anti-global warming campaign during Advent, the Christian liturgical season that awaits the birth of Jesus. Several parishes like Saint Luke's in Westborough and Saint Susanna's in Dedham have already committed to environmentalism. Why not enlist them for three weeks of prayer vigils at an Exxon gas station?

My brother-in-law Eric Schaeffer, former chief law enforcement officer at the Environmental Protection Agency and current executive of the Environmental Integrity Project, once told me that all the oil companies are bad, but Exxon is the worst of the worst.

"If you were in the middle of a vast desert on an emergency mission to reach a hospital and the only gas station available was Exxon, it might be morally acceptable to buy their gas," Eric said, "but not otherwise."

A penitential season with a joyful undertone, Advent lends itself to hopeful reform. Churches use the symbol of an evergreen wreath with four candles to mark progress toward Christmas. Three of the candles are penitential purple, but one, reserved for the third Sunday in Advent is joyful pink. Called Gaudate Sunday, it might be a fine day to declare carbon-free or as near as possible. We could use the first two weeks of Advent to build awareness and then nonviolently block entrances to the station with banners while citing the motto of Pope Francis and the Movement for the Abolition of Wars: "War Causes Climate Change, Climate Change Causes War."

In a 2004, a Catholic Worker Peace Team to Darfur, Sudan, included Brenna Cussen, Chris Allen-Douçot, Grace Ritter, and me. We saw firsthand how climate change depleted water, fueled genocide, and caused mass migration. We have a responsibility to link the use of gasoline in the United States with suffering elsewhere. A night in police lockup, a trial, and, perhaps, a short jail sentence might inspire us and, perhaps, our sisters and brothers to escalate environmental protection.

But, I am, once again, getting ahead of myself, and must admit that even Martin, with his activist passion, isn't a one-note piano. His seemingly altruistic decision to drive the entire seven-hour route to London had an ulterior motive: he wanted to be sure to arrive in time for Tottenham to face Leicester in Premier League Football. A longtime Tottenham fan, Martin, like many Brits, is passionately loyal to his team.

When I learned Martin was a soccer fan, I remembered Phil Berrigan telling me that professional sports mindlessly distract from our primary duty to work for nuclear disarmament. Phil's laser focus on peacemaking caused me to want to ask, "Hey, Phil, what will you do after the revolution?" Only later did I discover that his guilty pleasure was watching James Bond movies.

Interestingly, Martin's team, Tottenham (pronounced "Tott-num," by locals) arch-rivals my son Patrick's favorite, Arsenal. Although Patrick lives in Durham, North Carolina, where he teaches middle school while his wife, Jun, works on her doctorate in environmental science at Duke University, he follows Premiere League Soccer more than US sports. Apparently, Arsenal has 113 million fans worldwide. When I visited him in February, Patrick took me to a pub at seven in the morning where Arsenal fans packed in to watch a live broadcast of a match against Tottenham. Fans bedecked themselves with red and white Arsenal jackets, hats, shirts, and scarves, in an electric atmosphere.

All of a sudden, a leader yelled, "What do we think of Tottenham?"

The crowd roared, "SHIT!"

The leader asked, "What do we think of shit?"

"TOTTENHAM!" they replied.

He shouted, "Thank you!"

And they all said, "That's all right. We hate Tottenham, we hate Tottenham, we hate Tottenham, we hate Tottenham. We are the Tottenham haters!"

They followed with a Christmas carol:

> Away in manager,
> no crib for his bed,
> the little lord Jesus jumped up and said,
> "We hate Tottenham!

> We hate Tottenham!
> We hate Tottenham!
> We hate Tottenham!
> We are the Tottenham haters!"

In a reference to the fact that Arsenal beat Tottenham in their previous home stadium, White Heart Lane, the fans chanted:

> We won the league at Shite Heart Lane.
> We won the league at Shite Heart Lane.
> We won the league at the shit hole.
> We won the league at Shite Heart Lane.

And then, recalling that the last time Tottenham defeated Arsenal for the trophy, they yelled:

> You won the league in black and white,
> you won the league in black and white.
> You won the league in the sixties,
> you won the league in black and white.

In the interest of fair play, I looked up some anti-Arsenal chants, and they did not disappoint. The tamest one, sung to the tune of something called "The Little Birdie Song" says:

> He's only a poor little Gunner [an Arsenal fan].
> His wings are all tattered and torn.
> He made me feel sick
> so I hit him with a brick.
> Now he don't sing any more.

Another that begins with "My old man said, 'Be an Arsenal fan,'" crosses too many lines for me to include the rest.

In reference to a 1991 playoff victory over Arsenal, Tottenham fans chant:

> We beat the scum three to one, three to one
> We beat the scum three to one!

Clearly, there is no love lost between the fans of either team.

When all was said and done, though, despite the enthusiasm of Patrick and his friends in Durham, Tottenham won the game five to four.

As a Massachusetts native, I scoured the English papers without success for news of the Boston Celtics' quixotic post-season struggle to beat the highly-favored Cleveland Cavaliers. Apparently English football eclipses everything.

After dropping off Richard outside Dover, Martin navigated the way to Giuseppe Conlon Catholic Worker house on Mattison Road in north London. The community occupies a former church and next door vicarage on one of ten parallel residential streets perpendicular to a busy road lined with restaurants and shops. Because Mattison and the other nine streets ascend a hill, they are popularly known as The Ladder.

Shortly after our arrival, Alma left for Sweden, Clive for Oxford, and Martin for Wembley Stadium while I took an exploratory 6.8-mile run about the neighborhood. As I passed Turkish, Indian, and Chinese eateries, I considered what I had learned about Red Hand: I knew him as a highly educated and smugly argumentative, Catholic, trash-talking, middle-aged runner who follows me around the world. He may or may not have survived being stabbed by Don Banes, whom he may or may not have caused to suffer a heart attack.

Even more speculatively, Red Hand may orchestrate spooky side-effects like turning lights on and off, making strange sounds, and grabbing me from under the bed, although it remains much more likely that my runaway imagination concocted those phenomena. In any event, I hoped, as Shakespeares' Richard II did, that

.... this fortress built by Nature for herself against infection and the hand of war; this happy breed of men, this little world; this precious stone set in the silver sea, which serves it in the office of a wall or as a moat defensive to a house against the envy of less happier lands; this blessed plot, this earth, this realm, this England

can keep me safe.

Monday, May 14

I joyfully explored the London Catholic Worker, an amazing warren. The narrow-halled vicarage reminded me of passages in the Saint Benedict and Mary Harris Catholic Worker row houses in Washington, DC, where I fell in love with Claire. Cozy bedrooms for volunteers and guests abound as well as two baths and a living room that opens onto a tiny back yard, fitted with a clothesline, chairs, a table, two raised garden beds, a statue of the Virgin Mary, an icon of Mary, and a garden hose.

A side door from the vicarage opens into an alley filled with bicycles. The church basement hosts a repair shop not unlike Worcester's Earn-A-Bike giveaway program. The alley is shielded from the elements by a corrugated roof under which a string of Christmas lights provide nighttime illumination. A chicken-less chicken coop sits on a low, flat, rear section of the vicarage's roof. Mirjam told us that, when the birds didn't thrive, the CW gave them to a rural family and transformed the coop into a greenhouse.

A short stairway leads into the church hall with three long tables set up for meals. Couches arrayed around a television provide places for watching three hours each evening. Children's peace art hanging from a clothesline decorates the space with its several yellow stained-glass windows. A balcony above the adjoining kitchen houses more guest rooms. The community hosts eighteen refugees, but you'd hardly know it, the space is so varied.

Mirjam introduced us to community members Roland and Ghazal. Twenty-something and a slender man with a warm smile, Roland could easily stand in for the Irish actor, James

Nesbitt of *Bloody Sunday*[74], *Millions*[75], *The Way*[76], and *The Hobbit*[77] movies fame. Ghazal, a very bright and gregarious Muslim, has a law degree. Her Pakistani parents wish she followed a career track instead of helping shelter refugees and attending peace vigils.

In an article Ghazal wrote about voluntary poverty, she quotes Nora:

> Because we are able to work for free here—as a community—we can support the people who for political reasons aren't getting support. So, I see our work as resistance to capitalism, to the hostile environment of policy, and I feel very privileged that I have the freedom to do this. I feel like I am free to do the work that is important to me, because I don't have to worry about finding someone who will pay me for it.

Ghazal goes on to say:

> What makes Giuseppe Conlon House and other houses of hospitality different to a night shelter is that those who are welcomed—whether refugees or homeless people or anybody else—are not treated as 'service users' as in the vernacular of many charities; they are 'guests.' They live together with volunteers in an intentional community in which friendships can develop between guests and volunteers. Guests also move out of the house whenever they are ready.... The government has austerity measures and the Catholic Worker movement has teachings of dignity and that every person is Christ.

At breakfast, I met a charming man, Cecil, who sounded like he was from the Caribbean. I also met Paul, an American former oil company employee. I couldn't tell if Cecil and Paul were Catholic Workers or guests, an ambiguity that spoke highly to me of the community's values.

After I finished eating, I meandered into the church proper with several predominantly yellow stained-glass windows overlooking Mattison Street. Originally Methodist and then Catholic, the church closed years ago. Martin persuaded the bishop to give it and the vicarage to the Catholic Worker. Unlike any church I've seen in the United States, it's equipped with two front doors instead of one central set. The doors lead to a sanctuary below a cascading half circle of pews, a little like a nineteenth century lecture hall. Canned goods, dry food, blankets, clothes, suitcases, and peace banners are stacked up on the pews.

A pipe organ is set into the righthand wall while a piano sits on the floor to the left of the altar. The church floor has no-nonsense blue-grey carpeting. The sanctuary, adorned with a wooden crucifix, has a red carpet and a maroon back wall. A white cloth with gold embroidery on the edges covers the altar, which has candles and a faded icon of Jesus along with images of Mary, Saint Francis, Dorothy Day, and Christ behind barbed wire. Four comfortable chairs with cushions face the altar in a semicircle.

At 9 A.M., I took one of those seats for morning prayer made up of Taizé chant, a psalm and Gospel reading, twenty minutes of silent meditation, intercessions, and the Lord's Prayer. Nora sat to my left. With her long black hair and tiny nose ring, she wore a purple and red sweater, black jeans, and an ankle bracelet. She had bare feet, and I could also see her toenails painted blue. Paul, the American expatriate about my age at my right dressed conservatively. Claire sat on the far left beside Nora. Mirjam and Roland had business elsewhere.

Perhaps due to laziness, I resolved that today I would not meditate. When Nora rang the mindfulness bell, instead of spiritual reflection, I plotted what I wanted to include in my journal but thought better of it. I decided to give the meditation a go.

After bumbling about a bit thinking of what I might see rather than waiting to actually see or not see something, I caught a glimpse of the difference between giving my imagination free reign and making myself a blank slate. Just about to give up, I saw the dark wall of the void and impulsively dove headfirst into it.

Now you have to understand that diving ranks high up on the list of my phobias. While I understand intellectually that I could master the technique if I could relax, my body refuses to cooperate. When I get on an actual diving board, my muscles grow tense as piano wire just as they do when I try to ice skate. I can *picture* myself smoothly plunging into a pool or gliding over a frozen pond, but it never works out that way. In the former situation, I painfully flop on my belly, and in the latter, I do so on my derrière. Save when I enjoy it from a drinking glass, water in its liquid and solid forms conspires to hurt me.

Today, I glided painlessly downward into the void with my arms at my side. Like a born swimmer, I arched upwards, propelling myself gracefully with my hands and feet, upon which I came to rest in a standing position. Shortly thereafter a wooden chair appeared. I sat down on it. A small table with a glass of water on a doily materialized to my right, followed by a comfy chair covered with a flowered bed sheet. Dressed in a long, homespun outfit, Jesus plopped down in the chair. He looked beat.

Without a word or glance in my direction, he took a drink, replaced the glass, and nudged it toward me. I reached for it only to see the formerly immaculate outside smeared with dirt, sweat, and blood. The discolored water didn't look very appealing either, but nonetheless, I apprehensively took a small sip. To my surprise, it tasted wonderful, the finest beverage I've ever had. After I replaced the glass, Jesus grinned, put something in my hand, and disappeared. When I opened my palm, I saw that the Son of God had given me a television remote control. At that very moment, Nora rang the bell signifying the end of meditation.

In marked contrast to our immersion in the day's spiritual beginning, Claire and I spent the meat of it on a walking tour called Darkest Victorian London. Initially skeptical of the outing, I was pleasantly surprised by how much social commentary it included.

With about twenty tourists and a guide calling himself Richard the Third, we began at the enormous memorial pillar to the 1666 Great Fire of London that incinerated the homes of seventy-thousand of the city's eighty thousand inhabitants while killing remarkably few people. Unlike the 1871 Great Chicago Fire, though, the British blaze did not make way for a more modern city.

Narrow streets prevailed in post-conflagration London. Each building had a basement cesspit with human waste collected by children lowered down each night with buckets. Wagons carried the feces away and disposed of it in farmers' fields before the sun came up. Inhabitants or their servants tossed urine out the window into the street with a warning cry of "gardyloo" from the French, "Regardez l'eau": "Watch out for the water." To this day, Brits call a toilet the loo.

Urine and dirty water flowed down to the Thames, which became an open sewer. Not until The Great Stink of 1858[78] did construction of a public sewerage system begin. Even after its completion, London had to contend with tens of thousands of tons of horse manure every day. Smoke from coal fires mixed with fog to produce a toxic and often impenetrable atmosphere. Add to those challenges a lack of affordable housing, low wages, scant public education, and no right to vote, and it's clear that London's poor suffered enormously.

Unlike the American propensity to refer to things like racism as a past problem now solved, our guide took pains to link Victorian poverty to modern London, where wages in gentrifying, formerly affordable neighborhoods do not keep pace with soaring expenses. As if to underscore our guide's point, we passed an advertisement for a three-bedroom apartment renting for $4,500 a month. Ironically, the flat was located near the site of a Victorian workhouse for the destitute.

Agreeing with Charles Dickens, Richard the Third detailed the horrors of Victorian workhouses so appalling that "many would rather die than go there." He showed us the wall of the debtors' prison where Dickens's father was incarcerated. In the rest of Europe, the maximum sentence a person could serve to expunge a debt equalled one year. The British Isle had no limit. A person stayed in jail until payment of his or her entire debt, plus interest, as well as the cost of incarceration. Some unfortunates spent thirty years behind bars for small debts.

When I heard those stories, I couldn't help but think about pay-day loans with massive interest rates and other scams that imprison today's American poor as surely as any Victorian jail.

Most moving of the entire tour, though, involved the Cross Bones Graveyard where Victorians unceremoniously dumped prostitutes, orphans, runaways, and other "Outcast Dead." In the early 2000s, a public campaign saved that portion of the Thames trendy South Bank from greedy developers. All along its wrought iron fence, hundreds of ribbons commemorate the names, birth and death dates, and personal information of many of the previously forgotten. Although the graveyard no longer accepts new burials, memorials to today's outcasts still festoon the fence.

Cross Bones Graveyard

My expectation that the tour would be a sentimental look at Victorian London evaporated when I saw the faces of children, women, and men among the ribbons. While a photographer under a hood using a phosphorus flash may have taken some and owners of smartphones may have taken others, they all evoked a happiness denied and life cut short.

Thankfully, our guide also took us to a neat set of brick cottages sitting behind a delightful garden. Established by a Victorian philanthropist, Octavia Hill, they provided afford- able housing beside an oasis of natural beauty, a mission that continues under the supervision of the British National Trust. Too often, clever lawyers find ways to circumvent provisions meant as perpetual and undo bequests of philanthropists, but not so with Hill's estate.

After the tour and a cup of coffee for Claire, we wandered along the banks of the Thames to Tower Bridge. I found it much more impressive than distinctly modern nearby build- ings erected in recent years. With practicality and gravi- ty-defying curves, newer structures seem to vie too eagerly for notice while simultaneously deserving it all the less. Even though it's actually a twentieth-century suspension bridge disguised as Victorian, Tower Bridge reminds me that older often wears better. Claire and I must confess that we both succumbed to the bridge's charm and posed for photos before and along it.

With time running out for us to meet Nora, Roland, Mirjam, and Ghazal at Giuseppe Conlon House, I suggested we descend at the bridge's north end to a path alongside The Tower of London toward the Bank Underground station. In a corner of the stone stairway down to the bank of the Thames lay the crumpled form of a homeless man atop some filthy blankets. While I continued down the stairs, Claire paused to drop a couple of pounds into a cup set out for donations. When I noticed Claire was not at my side, I turned back and saw the vagrant gaze up at her. She may have said something to him. He had the kind of fleeting look on his face that makes me wish I had my camera at the ready. His eyes and smile reminded me of a portrait by Jusepe de Ribera that hangs in the Worcester Art Museum. His remarkable expression certainly constituted a greater gift than whatever Claire left in his cup.

Two hours later found us having tea in the cozy front parlor of Bruce Kent and his wife, Valerie Flessati, in their home not far from the Catholic Worker. Friends of our dear friend Michael True, Bruce and Valerie have been peace activists for more than sixty years. Bruce helped Giuseppe Conlon house get started. Although no one offered cucumber sandwiches, the tea felt very English.

A bit hard of hearing, Bruce radiated good cheer. Valerie, in a rainbow peace scarf, was charmingly hospitable. They both asked more questions of us than we put to them. After tea, they escorted Nora, Roland, Mirjam, Ghazal, and us to a garden and trim lawn in a space no larger than our front room at Saints Francis and Thérèse Catholic Worker. Surrounded with rhododendrons, marigolds, and a statue of a dwarf Bruce called Grumpy Dane, we posed for a photo.

I told Bruce and Valerie that the night before, Martin, Claire, and I went to Mass at Saint Mellitus Church where we were impressed to see a shrine to the World War II Austrian conscientious objector Franz Jägerstätter[79]. After confessing that they had a hand in it being there, Bruce and Valerie invited us to join them at a noon vigil to commemorate conscientious objectors. Decades older than Claire and me, neither Bruce nor Valerie had given up activism.

To cap the evening off, Claire and I spoke at Friends House, a Quaker complex in central London, and then enjoyed a South Indian dinner. All and all, we had a full day with not a single encounter with Red Hand: just fine and dandy, as far as I'm concerned.

Tuesday May 15

While waiting for Claire outside the Catholic Worker house, I surveyed the neighborhood. All two- or three-storied brick affairs, the houses have white-trimmed windows, unique decorative facades, and enclosed backyard gardens. The South Harringay School, directly across the street, has an ivy-covered fence and ornamental gates, one with the word *GIRLS* chiseled on top and the other, *INFANTS*. I wondered if that commented somehow on the immaturity of boys.

Two yellow plastic sandwich boards set up in the street mark the area as a no-parking zone. On one side, they proclaim, "*THINK!* Save the air. Walk there."

In the playground beyond the gates, nine- or ten-year-old children run in all directions. Evidently heedless of their racial and religious differences, they make a delightful din. Climbing up and down a slide, kicking rubber balls, and playing four square, girls in headscarves mix easily with the others.

I thought of those children at the noon vigil in Tavistock Square, where organizers read aloud the names and circumstances of more than eighty past and present conscientious objectors. For each person who refused to go to war, vigilers laid a flower on a memorial established in 1994 not far from a statue of Mahatma Gandhi. At the reading of Franz Jägerstätter's name, I could only marvel that he refused conscription into Hitler's army despite the fact that his family, parish priest, and bishop pleaded with him to accept conscription.

A man with only an eighth-grade education, Jägerstätter said he had a dream that everyone was boarding a train speeding toward Hell, a train he could not ride in good conscience. "Let us love our enemies, bless those who curse

Franz Jägerstätter

us, pray for those who persecute us," he said. "For love will conquer and will endure for all eternity. And happy are they who live and die in God's love."

Beheaded in 1943, Jägerstätter was beatified in 2007. Such faith, clarity, and courage deserves honor and notoriety.

Following the vigil, Claire staked out a comfortable spot beside the Friends House café so she could read and write, while I explored more of London. In my two-and-a-half-hour walk, I passed Bedford Square, inspiration for the title of an Anne Perry Victorian mystery, and entered the theater district where Harry Potter and the Cursed Child is running alongside older musicals like Chicago.

Union Jacks festooned Piccadilly Circus, perhaps in preparation for the wedding of Prince Harry and Meghan Markle. A street musician with a lovely voice drew a large crowd but few donations in his open guitar case. A band of young rockers, inexplicably wearing ski masks despite the eighty-degree heat, belted out a very credible rendition of the Kings of Leon song "Use Somebody."

As I kept walking, I couldn't help but sing,
I've been roaming around,
always looking down

drawing by Aiden Duffy

and all I see,
painted faces fill
the places I can't reach.
You know that I could use somebody.
You know that I could use somebody:
Someone like you.

It's a gift to hear and sing a love song on the streets of one of the world's largest cities.

I like to sing out loud while walking. As toddlers, my children adored that habit and as teens, abhorred it. As someone weaned on musicals where characters burst out into song just about anywhere, I found it natural to graduate from humming to full-on public singing, although I am too self-conscious to break into dance. God willing, though, I will one day kick my heels up like Gene Kelly in *Singin' in the Rain*[80].

As I neared Friends House, I passed University College, a venerable institution founded in 1826. Despite its impressive pedigree, I couldn't help wonder about its odd name. Calling itself "University College" seems vaguely oxymoronic and definitely unimaginative. If it's acceptable to say nation-state, I suppose one can get away with University College. After all, in *Animal House*[81], John Belushi proclaims his academic affiliation with a sweatshirt that says, without adornment, *COLLEGE*.

What I find unacceptable, though, were a number of posters slapped on lampposts around the neighborhood asking, "Why does Israel kill Palestinians?" However well-meaning the originators were, Israel is a country. Palestinians are a people. Unless Palestinians are allergic to the Jewish state, Israel cannot kill them. Israelis constitute another story altogether. Sad to say, many of them do kill Palestinians. And some Palestinians kill Israelis, too, for that matter. In fact, Israeli soldiers killed sixty Palestinians demonstrating against the Israeli-Egyptian blockade of the Gaza Strip this week. It's the latest chapter in decades of violence inflicted much more heavily and regularly on Palestinians than Israelis. While I share indignation over injustice and a passion for peace, this being England, the source of my mother tongue, I am also compelled to speak up for proper English syntax.

When I returned to Giuseppe Conlon House, Mirjam confessed that, while she liked my talks, she had to admit that she didn't feel as much joy in the Catholic Worker as I do. I'm glad she shared her sentiment with me, because I don't want to give the impression that I'm never annoyed, frustrated, bored, or angry. I told her about one night at Saint Benedict's Catholic Worker in Washington, DC, when I felt so burned out that I decided to stay outside until I could conclusively say I preferred going in.

As I began to shiver on that cold and rainy night, I said to myself, "It's still better out here." Not until thirty minutes passed and my co-worker Carl Siciliano opened the door to ask what I was doing did I go inside.

Everyone gets discouraged. At such times, another community member like Carl, can help big time. At other times, discouragement may signify a need to make changes in how we work or even to seek entirely new work.

"Although guilt did make the Irish nation," I told Mirjam, "no one should remain a Catholic Worker because of it. God wants us to be joyful—different from happy and very different from giddy. We need to be at once kind to ourselves *and* willing to make sacrifices for others. The first without the second amounts to hedonism, while the second without the first is self-destructive."

Awareness of human need can consume us. Thank goodness for Psalm 46, which says, "Be still and know that I am God." I interpret that as a divine command not only to pray but also to take breaks, sleep late, stroll by the sea, go to the movies, dance, fall in love, play with children, and enjoy a million other things now and then without feeling guilty.

And so, as the sun sank low on the horizon, I left Giuseppe Conlon house for a run. Turning right outside the front door, I took another quick right off Mattison Road into an alleyway called the Harringay Passage. Bisecting the Ladder's parallel streets, the flagstone passage extends almost all the way to Finsbury Park, where I ran previously. If I stretched out my arms to their full extension, my fingertips could touch the sides of the passage. Fifty-foot tall windowless brick facades of the houses gave way to shorter backyard barriers and another set of windowless walls followed by a cross street. Lit by three old-fashioned street lamps, the passage reminds me of colonial Boston.

After traversing four segments, I wound my way into the park and headed for a gem called the Parkland Walk. A runner's, biker's, and pedestrian's delight, the Parkland runs for a mile as a raised path with woods cascading down each side, creating the illusion that you are inside a forest instead of a major European city. Birdsong takes the place of car horns. If I didn't know better, I might think I ran on the West Boylston, Massachusetts, rail trail.

Unfortunately, however inviting the course, my body had not yet fully recovered from the marathon. Each day, a different segment cried out in pain. Today, the right side of my groin complained. The discomfort sufficed for me to turn back a bit early and actually walk the final half mile through the passage.

After sunset, clouds moved in and made it quite dark. When I entered the first segment of the passage, I felt grateful for the street lamps. As I walked along, I noticed the walls to people's back yards topped with a mixture of ivy, inlaid shards of broken glass, and barbed wire. As idyllic as the neighborhood appeared to be, break-ins apparently still caused concern.

I saw no one as I crossed Ducket Street, reentered the passage, crossed Cavendish, went back through the next segment of the passage, and then crossed Burgoyne, the last

drawing by Aiden Duffy

Harringay Passage

street before Mattison. As I entered the passage again, I began to feel chilled, something not uncommon for me after running.

The feeling deepened as I neared midway, and then, quite suddenly, I heard a popping noise behind me. When I turned, I saw that a lamp had burned out, something that didn't disturb me, since others shone brightly ahead of me. Unfortunately, two more popped off in succession, forcing me to stop completely while my eyes adjusted. Save for a bit of ambient city light above and at the end of the alley, I couldn't see a thing. If there had been a cinder block in my path, I'd have tripped over it.

Given my lights-out experience at the Phelan Center, I felt disconcerted. Still, darkness in the midsection of the passage amounted to considerably less than what enveloped either end between the windowless walls. I froze in place. Effectively, if anyone wanted to do me harm, I had trapped myself. While the distance wasn't long, I had no desire to run headlong into the pitch black despite my rosy experience during meditation. After all, that was a spiritual, even metaphorical thing, and this was a brick and mortar reality. As I didn't relish waiting there until dawn, I cautiously approached the inky gauntlet only to trip onto the flagstones.

"You okay, mate?" a friendly voice asked.

Looking up, I felt relieved to see someone in a Manchester United jersey reaching out to help me up. Somewhat embarrassed, I took his outstretched hand and regained my feet.

Just then, the clouds broke slightly to reveal the face of the man Don Banes tried unsuccessfully to stab to death.

Lost for words, I saw him withdraw his hand, pat me on the shoulder, and advise, "Be careful" before he strolled past me toward Finsbury Park.

After he melded into the darkness, the street lamps above me and all the others in succession came back to life.

The controversial villain had stalked me across the Channel! But, I had one consolation. I finally had allies. The only thing Tottenham and Arsenal fans hate worse than each other is Manchester United.

Traveling 477 miles an hour 38,000 feet above the Atlantic in a British Air jet that I can confirm from personal inspection does not harbor my nemesis—unless of course he is the pilot or copilot—I just enjoyed two movies. The first, *Marshall*[82], recounts a civil rights case US Supreme Court Justice Thurgood Marshall took on as a young lawyer in the 1940s. The second, *Downsizing*[83], concerns people who get themselves permanently shrunk down to five inches high in order to reduce their carbon footprint and enjoy a more luxurious lifestyle. Although it describes itself as a comedy, it includes a scientist's grim prediction of humanity's extinction by one means or another. His pessimism reigns as absolute as Thurgood Marshal's confidence that justice will prevail.

Two days ago, I finished *Magpie Murders*. Without spoiling the novel, I can tell you that the book offers a clever contemporary story wrapped around a fictional mystery novel called *Magpie Murders* set in the 1950s. The book's editor is the protagonist. By degrees, and often using instincts gleaned from years of editing mysteries, she tries to solve a murder the authorities ruled a suicide. After accumulating considerable evidence to back up her suspicion, she arranges a meeting with the detective assigned to the case. She presents her findings and he replies:

> What people don't seem to understand is that you've got more chance of winning the lottery than you have of being murdered. Do you know what the murder rate was last year? Five hundred and ninety-eight people—that's out of a population of around sixty million! In fact, I'll tell you something that may amuse you. There are some parts of the

country where the police actually solve more crimes than are committed. You know why that is? The murder rate's falling so fast, they've got time to look into the cold cases that were committed years ago.

I don't understand it. All those murders on TV—you'd think people would have better things to do with their time. Every night. Every bloody channel. People have some sort of fixation. And what really annoys me is that it's nothing like the truth. I've seen murder victims. I've investigated murder . . People don't plan those things . . . They don't put on wigs and dress up like they do in Agatha Christie. All the murders I've ever been involved in have happened because the perpetrators were mad or angry or drunk. Sometimes all three . . . .

Do you know why people kill each other? They do it because they're out of their heads. There are only three motives. Sex, anger, and money. . . . All the murderers I've met have been thick as shit. Not clever people. . . . And you know how we catch them? We don't ask clever questions and work out that they don't have an alibi, that they weren't actually where they were meant to be. We catch them on CCTV. Half of the time, they leave their DNA all over the crime scene. Or they confess. Maybe one day you should publish the truth, although I'm telling you, nobody would want to read it.

The detective might as well cite Ecclesiastes, "What has been will be again, what has been done will be done again; there is nothing new under the sun."

To the detective, life is mundane, humdrum, repetitive . . . boring. He might evokes Hemingway's analogy[84] that human beings are ants scurrying on the end of a burning log. Armed with statistics and experience, self-proclaimed realists like that detective throw ice water on the hopes of dreamers whom they regard as, at best, pathetic and, at worst, dangerous.

If he were an actual person, I would tell that detective a story from my youth. When I was fifteen, I put my moderately valuable coin collection in a small chest and hid it in a cave a half mile into nearby woods along with a note telling whoever discovered it, "This treasure is yours to keep. Do good with it."

Three days later, the police came to my door saying the parents of a boy, who found the chest, turned it in until its proper owner could be located. The cops first stop was my house. Apparently, my eccentricity was already common knowledge, just as the boy's parents were completely unwilling to admit, despite seeing it with their own eyes, that buried treasure does in fact exist.

Since then, I've learned that some people really do have adventures. In fact, more than a few sacrifice their lives for others like the hero in *A Tale of Two Cities*. Lovers cross mountains to be united. Treasures are discovered. Mysteries are plumbed. Life, while often uneventful and random, can also be every bit as exciting as the most imaginative fiction.

I would argue life can be an adventure, something most people want it to be. My son Aiden and his role-playing comrades don't traipse the woods pretending to be zombie killers solely because they're immature. They also do so because they yearn for adventure and haven't lost faith that such things actually exist. In *Galaxy Quest*, geeky sci-fi nerds glean expertise from computer games that saves the day. In

Tremors[85], when a gun-hoarding survivalist kills a graboid[86], Kevin Bacon says, "Guess we don't get to make fun of Burt's lifestyle anymore."

In *The Lost Boys*, the Frog brothers, using information they acquired from comic books, defeat vampires. In film after film, from *Miracle on Thirty-Fourth Street*[87] to *The Polar Express*[88], Santa Claus turns out to be real. We don't just hope there is more to life. Deep down, we *know* there is. My experience flying in a dark void simultaneously with sitting in the sun by a lake leads me to believe the fantastical is more than possible. It's imminent.

And so, like Bradley Cooper in *Silver Linings Playbook*[89] when he comes to the end of a bummer like *A Farewell to Arms*[90], I want to shout, "The world's hard enough as it is, guys. It's fucking hard enough as it is. Can't somebody say, 'Hey, let's be positive. Let's have a good ending to the story?'"

Chris's exasperated query to me in the Dortmund pub, "How can you be so fucking optimistic?", pertains.

Perhaps more intimately than some, I know that there is inexplicable suffering against which my efforts are slight, and yet Chris is right. I am optimistic. I reject the notion that we endlessly march over a cliff or pedal pointlessly on a stationary exercise bike. Sartre looks at a tree and feels existential nausea while I feel exhilaration.

In contrast, my friend Ken Hannaford-Ricardi says, "The glass is neither half full nor half empty. It's cracked right to its base." Like the scene in Woody Allen's *Annie Hall*[91], many of us complain "The food at this place is really terrible," and others add, "Yeah, I know; and such small portions."

While I suspect that most people who've spent time in hellholes— jails, ghettos, war zones—would agree with Thomas Hobbes's assessment that life is "nasty, brutish, and short," I do not.

Why?

Some of my attitude stems from personal experience with miraculous outcomes, some stems from familiarity with similar stories throughout history, and some of it comes from I have no idea where.

Years ago, I volunteered to run a late night errand for an acquaintance. My friend Kathy, who knew I was exhausted, asked me why I agreed to go. When I replied breezily, "Because it makes visible the Kingdom of God," she sobbed bitterly, "Why don't I feel like that?"

Old time Catholics fall back on the cliché, "It's a mystery," but I prefer to call it bloody unfair. It's one thing for human beings to deprive each other of life's necessities but another altogether to think that God rations grace.

When I encounter despair, I look to the heavens with balled fists and shout, "Open the spigot, for crying out loud!"

I've read Tolstoy's short story, "What Men Live By[92]." I understand that the divine plan is beyond me. I hear Saint Paul's assessment that we "see through a glass darkly," but I don't care. I want everyone I meet to feel like Cervantes's Man of La Mancha. I have no interest in being a flower among weeds. I want joy to be widespread, contagious. I want others to use me as a stepping stone to greater heights, a funny thing to write as our plane descends onto the tarmac in Boston.

Thursday, May 17

It's four in the morning, and I have been wide awake since three-thirty when I awoke from a vivid nightmare, shocking in its content and my clear memory of it. Typically, I can recall only snippets or general impressions of my dreams. Despite my best efforts to hold onto their narratives and imagery, details fall through my hands like sand on a windy day. This dream was different. My recollection is not cloudy at all, although I think I'd prefer that it were.

In the dream, Claire and I traveled with several others to Texas for some unknown reason. Our companions included a homeless man who believed he had been sent to earth from another planet.

Claire and I liked the fellow very much. His delusion not only seemed harmless but also prompted him to regard all manner of human behavior with fascination and delight. He'd see someone snap their fingers or whistle and exclaim, "Wow!" as if he'd witnessed some kind of miracle. Just as with our guest in Washington, DC, who thought he was Jesus, we treated the man as an actual visitor from another planet. He even looked a bit like Robin Williams from the seventies sitcom *Mork and Mindy*[93].

At one of our stops on the way to the Lone Star State, though, our typically jovial extraterrestrial sat with his head in his hands, a crumpled newspaper at his feet.

Uncharacteristically downcast, he said to me, "I'm so very sorry."

I sat next to him in concern and asked, "About what?"

"I haven't been entirely forthright with you," he confessed. "While it's true that I was sent here from my galaxy on an investigative mission, mine was not the first.

"My people have been watching humanity for many centuries with a mix of admiration and disgust. Nowhere in the universe have we seen a species so given to good and evil. Nonetheless, we were content to leave you be, even when you became capable of destroying all life on your planet.

"It was incomprehensible to us how you could be at once ingenious and remarkably short-sighted. So often you take perilous shortcuts with extremely high price tags rather than more difficult roads that lead to genuine solutions. You constantly put your faith in quick fixes like DDT, lead paint, asbestos, and plastic but always seem surprised when they inevitably bite you in the rear.

"Your proclivity to build ever bigger bombs rather than resolve conflicts confounds us. You could not stop yourselves from detonating a nuclear bomb even when your scientists suspected the chain reaction might destroy the earth. And then, while Hiroshima and Nagasaki were still in ruins, you fell for the lie that nuclear reactors would produce electricity 'too cheap to meter.'"

"Don't any of you read *Frankenstein*? For crying out loud, I'm not even from this planet, and I've read it! The only vision you seem capable of is hindsight. I cannot tell you how sad it was for us to watch you embrace idiocy over wisdom.

"And yet, we did not interfere. As horrifying as the prospect of your planetary destruction is for you, earth's destruction would have little impact on us.

"But your hubris didn't stop there. Like Icarus, you keep flying higher and higher, heedless of the consequences. And now, you have crossed the line. Instead of confronting global warming with renewable energy and conservation, you are hellbent on increasing growth, using more and more power, and ignoring Schumacher's spot-on critique in *Small Is Beautiful*[94].

"Sure. You've increased wind and solar power as well as recycling, but you won't give up pickup trucks, SUVs, heated pools, air conditioning, and consequent and obscene reliance on fossil fuels. You won't even give up leaf blowers! No, you want to have your cake and eat it, too.

"Your consumption orgy is not on the table for discussion, but as long as that's true, no number of windmills can produce enough energy. And so, once again, despite how often it has burned you in the past, you turn to a technological fix, a painless miracle cure.

"I won't get into details here. Suffice it to say, it's like cold fusion, infinite power for zero cost.

"If you had been paying attention when medieval scientists failed to turn lead into gold, you would object, but we are long past that. Your newest panacea, your energy salvation, will not only destroy your world but will also rip the fabric of the cosmos. Your foolish pride imperils the universe.

"This is something we cannot tolerate.

"And so, I have no choice but to recommend the enforcement of an injunction against you, an injunction that we have held in abeyance for many years."

"What kind of injunction?" I asked.

"One for your termination," he answered sorrowfully before continuing,

"Please understand that it gives me no pleasure to tell you this. I have always liked you, Claire, and many other humans as individuals. I've even been impressed with some of your social movements, but the sad truth is that good folks like you cannot stop the maniacs planning Armageddon. No, I'm afraid there is no other choice.

"For the greater good, your species must be exterminated."

"How long do we have?" I asked.

"A year, maybe two," he answered. "Take my advice. Spend time with your family. Enjoy the months you have left. As your guide book says, 'Eat, drink, and be merry, for tomorrow you die[95].'"

That's when I woke up.

I'm not much for dream analysis, but the peculiarly memorable and dire quality of that dream strikes me as so singular that I cannot dismiss it lightly. I feel like I just got spanked for spouting optimism.

Later in the day, Judith Flanders spanked me even harder. After my return from Europe, I grabbed her murder mystery, *A Howl of Wolves*, from the display shelf in the Worcester Public Library. How could I know that Flanders would choose, as Horowitz did, a female book editor as her narrator? Worse yet, an editor who complains about writers with "separation anxiety," "constantly wanting to rework a supposedly finished book"? And even worse, an editor who rolls her eyes at an author who believes a dream sequences adds gravitas to his or her novel? Yikes!

Synchronicity notwithstanding, I am reassured by a scene from Ron Howard's cable TV masterpiece, *Arrested Development,* where a psychiatrist named Tobias says to his estranged wife, Lindsay, that many couples tell him they try to save their failing marriages by dating strangers. When Lindsay asks how that goes, Tobias shakes his head. "It never works," he says. He pauses and brightens to add, "but in our case, it just might."

Besides, I actually had my dream, so it didn't occur as some trumped up literary device. I'm not that creative, believe me.

Friday, May 18

I guess lightning can indeed strike twice in the same spot. I've had another nightmare, and I remember this one, too. While Judith Flanders might say I'm like a dog going back to its vomit, I insist on sharing it with you. After all, as Oscar Wilde said so well, "Nothing succeeds like excess."

The dream opened with me standing in a creepy forest deep in a bayou. Gnarled trees draped with Spanish moss overhung a dirt path with pools of stagnant water on either side. After turning a bend, I saw a classic haunted house complete with a widow's walk and sagging front porch.

Against my better judgment, I approached and entered the creaking front door to find myself in a room crowded with furniture covered with dusty white sheets. From somewhere else, I heard a wailing cry.

My brain screamed, "Time to go," but my legs, contrary to their usual practice, insisted on investigating. They led me to a cellar door and, worse yet, down into the windowless basement where I could just make out an indistinguishable, dark figure in the corner with its back to me. The scene evoked *The Blair Witch Project*[96], a film that does not end well.

My terror had been mounting from the first moment of my nightmare but boiled over when I saw the figure stand, turn, and approach me. A quick backwards glance revealed that the stairway to safety had vanished.

I was royally screwed.

To make matters worse, the hooded specter lifted a bony hand to reveal its visage. Even though the fear of something horrible usually turns out much worse than the actual item, I was sure I faced an exception.

the classic haunted house of Scott's dream

To look in this creature's eyes would strike me dead with fright.

Quite suddenly, I had an insight and said, "I am not afraid."

The monster froze.

I went on, "I know who you are."

As if on cue, lights came up to reveal that my adversary was not just any man but a chagrined Red Hand, to whom I said, "I can guess your name."

"Thanks for nothing, Mick Jagger," he replied.

"Yes," I went on, "you are the Devil, Satan, The Lord of the Flies, Beelzebub, Old Scratch . . . "

"Yah, yah, yah," he interrupted. "Congratulations, Smarty Pants."

"You not only have many names, but you can show up anywhere."

"What can I say?" he shrugged with false modesty, "They don't call me legion for nothing, after all."

Seizing my advantage, I pressed on, "I'm no longer afraid of your parlor tricks—lights on/lights off, spooky noises, chills down the spine—either."

"Hey," he said. "Give me a break. I haven't used those gags in ages. Even a pro gets rusty, you know."

"By the way," I couldn't resist asking, "are you making some kind of political statement by appearing as an English-speaking white male?"

He brightened.

"I'm glad you picked up on that," he said. "Of course, I can and have appeared in many guises. For the time being, though, white privilege works for me."

"And also," I asked, "what was up with you taking Communion?"

"Oh, that," he chuckled. "While I don't want to weigh in on your Catholic/Protestant squabbles, I generally play it safe regarding the question of transubstantiation."

"But I saw you take Communion," I said.

"You saw the priest put it in my palm," he replied, "and presumed I took it. Again, I've got no horse in the race between denominations, but I must confess the wafer did sting quite a bit before I tossed it."

"Nonetheless," I said pointing my index finger at him, "you are singularly unimpressive."

"Now, here I must disagree," he said. "As a movie buff, you of all people have to admit that I am a vastly more interesting character than that lame-ass God of yours.

"Think about it. Actors and audiences adore me: Robert DeNiro in *Angel Heart*[97], Al Pacino in *The Devil's Advocate*[98], Tim Curry in *Legend*[99], Jack Nicholson in *The Witches of Eastwick*[100], Viggo Mortensen in *The Prophecy*[101], and Elizabeth Hurley in *Bedazzled*[102]. Trey Parker even portrays a credible me in *South Park*[103]. What have you got to compare? George Burns in *Oh God*[104]. Puh-leeze! Face it, the public knows I'm sexier than your guy.

"Musicians are onto this truth too. Kanye West had it right:

> You can rap about anything except for Jesus
> That means guns, sex, lies, videotape.
> But if I talk about God,
> my record won't get played.[105]'

"You've got nothing to compare with Black Sabbath, 'Bad to the Bone,' or 'Highway to Hell.' For Pete's sake, 'Sympathy for the Devil' is on the radio so often, you'd think it was the national anthem. I'd even be willing to wager on more bumper stickers saying, 'Dog is my co-pilot' than 'God is, etcetera.'"

"I can see this isn't going to be a short conversation," I observed. "Can we sit down while we talk?"

"I'm easy," he said snapping his fingers and settling into a velvet-cushioned throne that materialized on an elevated dais just before a wooden stool appeared behind me.

"Really?" I asked sarcastically.

"Don't blame me," he said. "You're the one who wasn't specific."

"Where was I?" he continued and answered his own question. "Oh yes, I'm sexy. But on top of that, I'm smart. In *Time Bandits*, David Warner played me just right when he said,

> God isn't interested in technology. He cares nothing for the microchip or the silicon revolution. Look how he spends his time: Forty-three species of parrots! Nipples for men! Slugs! *He* created slugs! They can't hear. They can't speak. They can't operate machinery. Are we not in the hands of a lunatic? If I were God, on day one, we'd have lasers!

"To quote Holland Taylor in *Spy Kids II*[106]," I retorted, "'Blah, blah, blah, I never understand a word you say.'

"I concede that the Hollywood God is unimpressive," I continued, "and, if you told me half the clergy works for you, I wouldn't be surprised, but that has little bearing whatsoever on the fact that the real Head Honcho, Big Cheese, Prince of Peace, and King of the Lanes is way cooler than you are on your best day in Vegas."

"Says you," he spat out. "But I've been watching pathetic chumps holding their breath for Jesus to come back while your merciless savior twiddles his thumbs in heaven. Unlike him, my stay wasn't a one-off house call. I never left. Personal appearances are my speciality and, as your buddy Don Banes discovered, I cannot be killed. I'm the Energizer Bunny from Hell. I go on and on."

"I'll grant you that," I said with a glance at my watch. "But even a TV show that gets renewed season after season can be a piece of crap. In fact, spending time with you verifies the old saying, 'familiarity breeds contempt.'"

"Sticks and stones . . . ," he countered.

"Fair enough," I nodded. "I accept that you can appear at will under a million disguises. I now know you can also butt into our dreams. You almost had me, by the way, when you appeared as an ecologist."

"Pshaw," he reddened. "I felt inspired."

"I also recognize that you aren't just sowing despair in individuals," I went on. "No, you are a mover and shaker. You insinuate yourself into movements and political parties of the Right, Left, and Center."

"Right again, Einstein," he said. "I especially enjoyed the symmetry of pushing segregation in the 1950s through Southern Democrats and now through Republicans. Mao's Cultural Revolution gave me a hoot too, if I do say so myself."

Ignoring his prattle, I said, "Even though you have caused enormous harm, have catapulted despots and dictators into power, and sustained them for decades, you can't win."

"What are you talking about?" he cried. "Cruelly oppressive Roman, British, Chinese, Russian, and Mughul empires lasted for centuries. The pitiful Camelot moments you've had in history cannot compare, not even with a short rule like the Nazis, because its impact reached so far. Think about it. You fought for centuries to stop slavery, to emancipate women, to end racism and war, but they go on and on. If that's not winning, I don't know what is."

"The reason you cannot win," I explained, "is that the deck is stacked against you. In order for you to claim victory, you have to corrupt every single human being. God only needs one faithful servant in order to continue loving humanity. Your Nazis nearly conquered the world, but Sophie Scholl and a bunch of other teenagers made fools out of them with the White Rose, just as Franz Jägerstätter, Sojourner Truth, and inspired people have made a fool out of you throughout history.

"God could wipe every tear away and, yet, chooses not to. To you, this proves indifference or impotence, but, like Dostoevsky, I believe God respects our free will too much to win our loyalty with the wave of a magic wand. God knows the impossibility of love without freedom and the risks of freedom. God refuses to enslave us. While you wield a grotesquely heavy hand and God treads lightly, your darkness cannot overcome the light."

"Freedom?" he spat. "Even Heidegger knew it was a burden."

"Martin Heidegger," I retorted, "was a Nazi."

"Hey," he lectured. "If you don't have something nice to say . . ."

Ignoring the childish remark, I continued, "The biggest fallacy in your spiel, the one I almost fell for, concerns the caricature of God as an absentee landlord. When I saw you dispensing hurt and fear, I wanted God to show up. I wanted miracles to eclipse your shenanigans. I lost sight of the fact that God doesn't speak through an earthquake, firestorm, or mighty wind, but in 'a still small voice.'"

"You need therapy," he interrupted. "You have an elaborate rationalization. Your God is no better than an imaginary friend, like that rabbit in *Harvey*[107]. I know your confirmation name is Thomas, but you can't possibly be gullible enough to fall for Saint John's Pablum, 'Blessed are those who believe without having seen.' No, I take you for a show-me-the-money kind of guy.

"Be reasonable," he continued. "Don't let stubborn pride keep you from facing the hard truth that the great pretender is not here on earth, while I very much am."

"You are indeed," I said. "But contrary to your propaganda, God has not left us by ourselves to flail in a shark tank. God is more present than you will ever be. Even my amateur forays into meditation prove it. Soul-satisfying comfort has always been at our finger tips. And more to the point, I'm going to tell Joan Osborne that Christ is at once a 'stranger on the bus' and 'a slob like one of us[108].'

"I didn't realize it at the time," I kept on, "but I put a euro into Jesus's hand in Dortmund and looked into his eyes on Tower Bridge. I drove him to the bank, where, out of a paltry disability check, he gave me a five-dollar bill and envelopes of cash for our guests Sean and John. Claire wiped up his precious blood from our bathroom floor. I also saw him in the European Catholic Workers, in the people at our weekly vigil, and at monthly evening prayer. I even saw him at the pub run."

"Metaphors," he sneered, "are poor substitutes for flesh and blood apparitions. Saying Christ is in the needy and saintly is no more comforting than saying, 'There's pie in the sky.'

If Jesus gave a damn, he wouldn't slink around in disguise. He'd reveal himself as I do. When I'm called, BINGO. I'm on the spot. Even Mother Theresa admitted that decades of her prayers went unanswered. Shusaku Endo had it exactly right when he titled his book about God *Silence*[109]."

The remark caught me off guard. When I hesitated, he leaned back in triumph.

"Admit it," he gloated. "You won't call on God to swoop down to your rescue because you 'must not tempt the Lord, your God,' *but* because you know he won't come. He didn't come for Sophie Scholl, and he's not coming for you, either."

As he spoke, darkness started reclaiming the surroundings, and his visage appeared more frightful, but as my ship began to flounder, I thought of Tolstoy's line, "In the midst of winter, I find within me the invisible summer." Was he insane to write *The Kingdom of God Is Within You* in czarist Russia? Could mystics be onto something? Is there an exhilarating spiritual reality not only within our grasp but encompassing us at all times? And even more to the point, did Rumi have it right to believe, "Love calls—everywhere and always"?

I looked up as Satan swelled to enormous proportions, taking on the form of a gigantic and ravenous spider, my greatest fear. Clearly, he intended to devour me without delay, but before his pincers could crush me, I reached into my pocket, pulled out the remote control Jesus gave me, pointed it at the beast, depressed the power button, and, POOF. He vanished.

At that instant, I woke completely refreshed.

Later on, I found a record-setting 92 cents on the ground to bring Claire and my retirement total up to $84.31.

Saturday, May 19

After evening prayer on Wednesday, our friend Kate Carew asked me about our trip to Europe. Among other things, I described rising anti-immigrant sentiment and formidable measures taken at Calais to prevent refugees from crossing the English Channel.

When I mused, "I wonder if soldiers would really shoot at families," she said, "They shot at one this morning and killed a two-year-old."

Yesterday, Kate forwarded me the story from the *Guardian*:

Authorities in Belgium have admitted that a two-year-old girl who died after police opened fire on a van carrying migrants near Mons on Thursday was shot in the face.

Prosecutors had initially denied the account given to the *Guardian* by relatives of the girl, called Mawda, suggesting instead that she had been taken ill or died as a result of erratic driving.

The child was killed after a police patrol followed and intercepted a van containing twenty-six adults and four children, including Mawda, on a highway near the city of Mons in the early hours of Thursday morning.

She was travelling with her Kurdish-Iraqi parents and three-year-old brother. A source told the *Guardian* that police opened fire in an effort to stop the vehicle, which was being driven by alleged people smugglers to a lorry park on the coast. From there, the refugees were to be smuggled on board lorries destined for the UK.

All I can think of is the anti-Vietnam War poster showing young casualties and asking, "And Children, too?"

Then, on Thursday, Claire and I attended the funeral for our eighty-eight-year-old African American neighbor Lula

Dyer at Mount Sinai Church of God in Christ. She was the daughter of sharecroppers. Lula and her husband, Reverend Douglas Dyer, moved to Worcester in 1964, where they raised children and grandchildren. Countless times since we opened Saints Francis and Thérèse Catholic Worker in 1986, either or both of them have helped us out. Lula's death, even at such a ripe age, leaves a hole in our hearts.

I expected a good deal of crying during the service, and there were tears, but far fewer than I imagined. Instead, a minister opened by saying, "I'm here to sing, shout, and dance," and he meant it.

The choir would have put James Brown to shame. Instead of dreading death, the singers proclaimed, "No more crying, no more dying" and "Don't you wanna to go?"

In her eulogy, Lula's daughter Sandra took fire, saying, "We gotta fight and soar like eagles!"

Accompanied by an electric guitar, organ, and full set of drums, the choir sang, "I am never alone" because "Jesus always walks beside me."

A different minister testified, "The bible tells us one can defeat a thousand! Hallelujah! The bible tells us one can defeat ten thousand! Hallelujah!"

The mourners paid death no more mind than I would a hiccup.

Then, this morning as I came out of the grocery store, I saw the mother of my son Justin's grade-school classmate Charlie Kaneb pull up in her 1999 Miata convertible with the top down despite cool weather. Wearing a jaunty cap, she waved to me before entering the store, but the dozens of bumper stickers covering her car on all sides transfixed me. Some of them said:

> Politics is the entertainment division of the
> military-industrial complex.
>
> —Frank Zappa

> Great minds discuss ideas. Average minds discuss events.
> Small minds discuss people.
>
> —Eleanor Roosevelt

> I like your Christ. I do not like your Christians.
>
> —Gandhi

> Don't believe everything you think.
> It only hurts when I stop dancing.
> There's no planet B.
> What wisdom can you find that is greater than kindness.
> Speak your mind, even if your voice shakes.
> March On.
> Caution: Driver is Singing.
> Reading is sexy.
> Fearful people do stupid things.
> A revolution without dancing is not worth having.
> There's enough to go around if everyone counts.

Disguised as an affable alien, Red Hand almost persuaded me that we are doomed. Like the Grand Inquisitor, the extraterrestrial dismissed humanity's capacity to sacrifice for others. My experience as a runner, where I know that pain yields gain, my day-to-day life, the example of the European Catholic Workers and Catholic Workers everywhere, and my visions (for lack of a better word) save me from despair. Without sentimentality, I am convinced that, if I am unafraid to dive into darkness, taking a risk for others, I can accomplish what love demands.

I don't think you have to be religious to have such faith. Just from reading her bumper stickers, I suspect Charlie Kaneb's mom is, in the deepest sense, very spiritual. Like Lula's congregation, Charlie's mom refuses to surrender to fear or hopelessness. She knows that living simply will not ruin our lives, our nation will not be overrun if we disarm, and our boat will not sink if we welcome refugees. After all, "There's enough to go around if everyone counts."

Sunday, June 17

Despite nocturnal reassurance bolstered by the faith I witnessed at Lula's funeral and on Charlie Kaneb's mother's car, nagging doubts persisted. After all, dreams, religious faith, and bumper sticker idealism may derive from delusion. I believe I had two visions of Christ and saw him in human disguise, but in the two months since I started this journal, Red Hand performed the only supernatural action I've witnessed. While I know Jesus is loath to enslave us to miracles, it would be nice to see a him turn a light on or off now and then.

In high school, I joined the debating team. Just to give myself a challenge, I always argued the more difficult proposition, but after I won a debate in defense of slavery and another in defense of the Spanish Inquisition, I decided that I should never become a lawyer because my drive to win superseded factual and ethical considerations.

Have I now locked myself into a theistic world view by making a case for God regardless of the facts? Was Red Hand correct that, deep down, I need to put my fingers in the Christ's wounds before I can truly believe? Like most mysteries, these play out in day-to-day life.

Three days ago, I got a call from a social worker who appealed for us to accept a heroin addict just released from jail. He did not want to risk his sobriety by staying in Worcester's wet shelter. With the same name as our son Justin, he came to our door with only the clothes on his back.

The following morning, I brought him some shirts, socks, and toiletries, for which he was grateful.

Minutes later, his roommate, an affable and hardworking guy named Jonathan came downstairs and told me, "I don't like to speak ill of anyone, but my new roommate is not a good guy. He told me he was a thief, and last night he was on the phone until two in the morning. I overheard him telling someone to meet him outside but to park around the corner so he would not be seen. He went outside and then went in and out of the bathroom for the next hour."

The obvious implication: Justin took advantage of our always open front door to score drugs. Flo, another genial guest, confirmed Jonathan's report, so I confronted Justin. Like every addict we've hosted, he vehemently denied being on drugs and offered to take a urine test as proof.

"I've been doing this work for thirty-two years," I told him. "Ninety-nine percent of the drug addicts we've hosted have said the same thing, and all of them lied. One overdosed. We cannot have any doubt about sobriety here not only for the sake of other guests who try to keep their sobriety, but also for your safety. too."

After reading him the riot act, I warned him that any future indication of drug use would result in our asking him to leave immediately. Although it often proves a mistake, we prefer to give our guests at least one and even two extra chances to stay within our minimal rules.

Yesterday when I returned from our monthly vigil against the American gun culture, I found our kitchen door ajar. I saw a half-full water glass on the table and called out to see if Claire had returned from baking cinnamon swirls. It surprised me when no one answered, but when I entered our middle room and saw the charging cord for Claire's watch on the floor, my spider sense tingled. Claire's laptop, which usually sits on an adjacent small white table, was missing. I feared someone had stolen it, something that Claire confirmed a few minutes later when she returned.

"Oh, no!" she moaned. "It has all my research and all my work for the Center [for Nonviolent Solutions] on it! Multiple tabs were open. All my photos are on it, too."

With an unlocked front door, you might think we'd get robbed quite often, but it rarely happens. In more than thirty years, thieves have taken things maybe six or seven times. Unfortunately, Claire has lost three laptops. In an attempt to preserve the last one, she installed anti-theft software, but that only led us on a wild goose chase of locations through which the laptop had passed without ever actually locating it. The police sympathized but said they virtually never recover laptops. Even if hers could be found, most likely the thief or thieves would have wiped all data.

Claire noticed two cigarette butts on a kitchen shelf. The thief had not only brazenly entered the house in broad daylight but had poured himself or herself a drink and had a smoke, too. Their apparent familiarity with the house made me suspicious that the culprit was a former guest and Claire suspicious that it was our current guest Justin.

Since I had been out of the house for less than two hours, Claire urged me to join her in a search for Justin. We drove around for a half hour without any luck. On our way back, I told my despondent spouse that the glass could have fingerprints on it to confirm whether or not the thief had been Justin or someone else. Neither of us had much confidence, though, that the police would dust the glass or anything else in our kitchen for fingerprints over the theft of a cheap laptop.

When we reached the CW house, Claire called the police. I went upstairs where I found Flo in the kitchen and, in the next room Justin lying on his bed talking on the phone.

"I'm going to be talking to everyone in the house," I said to Flo. "Claire's laptop was stolen today from the first floor. It's not worth much dollarwise, but it has all of her work on it. If you know anything about where it might be, please let us know."

Justin overheard me and came into the kitchen to express sympathy.

"The thief left a glass of water on the table," I told them both. "We're going to ask the police to dust it for prints."

"That's a good idea," Justin said. "They might be able to catch them that way."

His apparent sincerity led me to believe in his innocence. Claire felt less certain.

In any event, I had to leave to sell our bread before and after Mass at Saint Mary's Church in Uxbridge. With a heavy heart, I got into the car while Claire sat before my too-bulky-to-steal desktop computer to change the password for her email account. As I turned onto Chandler Street, I thought of stopping at a thrift store to see if someone had tried to sell Claire's laptop there but realized I didn't have time to do so.

As I drove down Route 146, I wondered if I could take some kind of spiritual response to the calamity. If it had been my computer, I could say, "Naked I came into the world, and naked I shall leave it," but I wasn't about to preach detachment to Claire.

When I arrived at Saint Mary's, I hauled all the racks of bread, muffins, and swirls inside and set up two tables, one in the front vestibule and the other in a back side entrance. As I did, I wondered if I might find inspiration in a vision, so afterwards, I sat down, closed my eyes, and tried to find the dark place.

Unfortunately, the church organist was practicing and I had a hard time emptying my mind. The closest I got to my inner world involved seeing an array of lights falling gently down like quiet fireworks. The display, while no help at all on specific action, comforted me.

I got up to bring a few of our newsletters to our bread table in the front vestibule. As I passed through the church, I noticed a side alcove with a statue of the Virgin Mary surrounded by votive candles. While many Catholics light candles to draw God's attention to their petitions, I rarely do so. Nevertheless, I thought, "What the heck. It couldn't hurt." I put five dollars in an envelope as an offering for a seven-day candle and knelt down.

Reason told me not to imagine that the thief would return the laptop, that the police would even look for it, or that Claire or I would find it, so I prayed, "Mary, your son went missing for three days in Jerusalem, but you found him in the temple. You can relate with Claire on losing something precious. Please use your pull with God to help Claire find her laptop."

To double the efficacy, I asked Dorothy Day to pitch in, too.

Throughout Mass, when tempted to accept that the laptop had vanished forever, I gently reminded myself of Saint John's advice that we should ask for things from God confidently, without doubts. I found it a pretty big leap, but having no other ideas, I went with it.

When I arrived back at our Mason Street home, Claire asked me to sit down and listen to what had happened in my absence.

"I went upstairs to question Justin again," she said. "I asked him if he had any idea where someone might sell a stolen laptop. He said most places won't buy a laptop unless they can be sure it's not stolen, but one place in the Midtown Mall does so with no questions asked."

Claire thanked him and then called our son Justin to see if he could give her a ride, since I had our car. Failing that, she called our daughter Grace and others, all without success, but then asked our guest Jonathan, who has a car, if he could drive her downtown. He agreed, and off they went. Jonathan promised to wait at the curb while she investigated.

Once inside the small, rundown, and very shady Midtown Mall, Claire discovered the shop Justin had mentioned way in the back. It had a note on the door, "Be back in ten minutes." A Latino stood with a bunch of DVDs which he may or may not have been trying to sell. Claire told him her quandary and, after introducing himself as Angel, he suggested she peer through the window.

"Can you see it?" he asked.

"No," she sighed.

He suggested she try a different store at the front of the mall which also buys laptops. Claire thanked him and went there.

After a woman at the door told her the owner did not buy laptops, Claire returned to the still-closed first shop, where Angel said, "Come with me. I know the guy."

He took her to meet the African-American owner who said he had just bought a laptop for fifty dollars. After Claire proved she knew the password and could unlock it, he agreed that it belonged to her. It had not been wiped of data. She was so delighted to have it back, she didn't mind at all giving the merchant the fifty dollars he would otherwise have lost in the transaction.

And so, Claire retrieved her laptop through the help of our guests Justin and Jonathan as well as a stranger named Angel.

I may be stubborn and skeptical, but such a miracle outdid all of Red Hand's antics. I knew once and for all that Red Hand was not the only person who cannot be killed. Jesus, his mother, and in all likelihood, Dorothy Day and other saints remain alive and willing to rescue us in a pinch, a revelation that really does call for fireworks.

a note from the author

Save the direct references to Red Hand, everything in this book actually occurred, including what seem like visions, my dream with the ecologist, and the concluding miracle.

I wrote the *The Man Who Cannot Be Killed* in real time with no advance knowledge of events that would take place. I'm pleased to say that Claire and my retirement fund has exceeded $123.13.

acknowledgments

Without a great deal of patience from my wife and co-worker, Claire Schaeffer-Duffy, I couldn't have written *The Man Who Cannot Be Killed.* I am grateful to all whom I quoted and spied on and then inserted into the text. My daughter Grace also provided helpful feedback and faithful support.

European Catholic Workers have earned my gratitude and admiration.

Scott Schaeffer-Duffy
runs the 2018 Providence Marathon

about the author

Scott Schaeffer-Duffy and his wife, Claire, have been Catholic Workers since 1982. They have four children and four grandchildren. Scott is author of *Nothing Is Impossible: Stories from the Life of a Catholic Worker*, 2016, Haley's, and *Murder on Mott Street: a Catholic Worker mystery*, 2018, Haley's. He plans to run the 2019 Boston Marathon. Scott welcomes reader questions and comments. He is available for talks, readings, and signings. Readers can contact him as follows:

Scott Schaeffer-Duffy
Saints Francis & Thérèse Catholic Worker
52 Mason Street
Worcester, MA 01610 USA
theresecw2@gmail.com

Aiden Duffy
finds his space in a Tuscan landscape

about the illustrator

Aiden Duffy studied art in Florence, Italy on his way to completing a degree in studio art from the College of the Holy Cross in 2016. He is an apprentice at Paulson Stained Glass in Upton, Massachusetts, and the assistant cross country coach at South High Community School, Worcester.

footnotes

[1]*Ironsides*-a television series set in San Francisco that ran from 1967-1975 starring Raymond Burr as Robert T. Ironside, a wheelchair-bound detective paralyzed from the waist down after being shot while on vacation. Despite its longevity, the series doesn't deserve a second look. For a detective with a disability, the protagonist in *House*, 2004-2012, is much better and funnier to boot.

[2]*Rear Window*-a fantastic 1954 Alfred Hitchcock murder mystery with Jimmy Stewart, recuperating from a broken leg, snooping on neighbors through a back window. Ironically, Raymond Burr, who later played only heroes, plays a villain. Remade in 1998, it starred the actually paralyzed actor Christopher Reeves. Like most remakes, it turned out just okay.

[3]*Marathon Man*-a must-see 1976 thriller starring Dustin Hoffman as a marathon-running graduate student who gets unwittingly mixed up in a diamond-smuggling ring. In the film's most terrifying scene, a Nazi war criminal played by Sir Lawrence Olivier tortures Hoffman with a dental drill. Roy Scheider, who just the previous year had killed the shark in *Jaws*, has a small role.

[4]*World War Z: An Oral History of the Zombie War*-the 2006 apocalyptic novel by Max Brooks that gave me the willies. The 2013 movie by the same title: not so much.

[5]*Zombie Survival Guide: Complete Protection from the Living Dead*-also by Max Brooks. What can I say? The title of this 2003 how-to book tells it all.

[6]*No Innocent Bystanders: Becoming an Ally in the Struggle for Justice*-co authored by Chris Allen-Douçot, one of the founders of the Hartford Catholic Worker and Shannon

Craigo-Snell, this excellent book considers how white people can make strides against racism.

[7]*Rosemary's Baby*-Mia Farrow stars in this 1968 film about a new mother's worst nightmare: that her child is the Antichrist and her husband, friends, and neighbors are his satanic allies

[8]*Invasion of the Body Snatchers*-a 1956 sci-fi classic film about a small town where sleeping humans are replaced by emotionless alien duplicates. The 1978 remake, starring Donald Sutherland, is pretty creepy too.

[9]*Farenheit 451*-Ray Bradbury's classic 1953 novel about a dystopian future when firemen burn books. It derives its name from the temperature at which book paper bursts into flame.

[10]Metric hour-fifty minutes (my book, my rules)

[11]*Nothing Is Impossible: Stories from the Life of a Catholic Worker*-a 2017, autobiographic masterpiece by Scott Schaeffer-Duffy. Excerpts, reviews, and comments by readers can be found at: *www.scottschaefferduffybooks.com*. Order your copy now at: *theresecw2@gmail.com*.

[12]"Herregud in himel!"-"Good God in Heaven!" in Swedish, as if you didn't already know

[13]*Wait Until Dark*-a 1967 thriller. Audrey Hepburn plays a blind woman who smashes the light bulbs in her apartment to gain an advantage over a would be murderer. Interestingly, Alan Arkin, who would go on to portray the hero in *Catch-22*, is the heartless bad guy.

[14]*Galaxy Quest*-a hilarious 1999 send-up of the *Star Trek* television series. Starring Tim Allen, Sigourney Weaver, the late great Alan Rickman, Sam Rockwell, and Tony Shalhoub,

it's a hoot. In the intro the Galaxy Quest television show, Tim Allen says, "As long as there is injustice, whenever a Targathian baby cries out, wherever a distress signal sounds among the stars, we'll be there. This fine ship, this fine crew. Never give up . . . and never surrender." If you haven't seen it, you must.

[15] *The Shining*-a 1980 horror movie starring Shelley Duval and Jack Nicholson that some consider a classic but I think is an overrated collection of disconnected horror tropes, unlike Stephen King's more coherent works, *The Dead Zone* and *Pet Sematary*

[16] *Sorry, Wrong Number*-a 1948 film noir mystery. Barbara Stanwyck plays an invalid who overhears a murder plot on the phone. Burt Lancaster plays the villain. The opening title card says: "In the tangled networks of a great city, the telephone is the unseen link between a million lives . . . it is the servant of our common needs — the confidante of our inmost secrets . . life and happiness wait upon its ring . . . and horror . . . and loneliness . . . and . . . death!"

[17] *Invasion*-a fine 2007 film starring Nicole Kidman that channels the *Body Snatcher* movies and wrestles with the pros and cons of free will. The only defense against alien takeover is staying awake. Coffee anyone?

[18] *The Stuff*-a 1985 gem of a movie about a new dessert sensation that literally takes people over

[19] *The Ring*-a 2002 American remake of the 1998 Japanese film of the same name. Everyone who views a certain video tape is doomed to a terrifying death with the week.

[20] *It's Alive*-a hard-to-believe-it-was-ever-made 1974 horror movie about a mass-murdering baby. This film gives new meaning to postpartum depression.

[21] *Gremlins*-a 1984 sci-fi, comedy, horror film. Adorable pets get transformed into malevolently mischievous monsters if, among other things, they get wet.

[22] *They Live*-John Carpenter's 1988 masterpiece movie. Magic glasses reveal the hidden identities of skeletal aliens pushing selfish-capitalism on earth. Canadian professional wrestler Rowdy Roddy Piper dons a pair of those sunglasses and sees that billboards actually say *CONSUME, WATCH TV,* and *OBEY.* Dollar bill embossments say *THIS IS YOUR GOD.* When Piper scans through the pages of what looks like a serious magazine with bar graphs, he sees *NO INDEPENDENT THOUGHT, STAY ASLEEP,* and *DO NOT QUESTION AUTHORITY.* If *The Man Who Cannot Be Killed* ever becomes a best seller, I'm going to order millions of those glasses for those Americans who still believe global warming is a hoax.

[23] *The Birds*-Alfred Hitchcock's 1963 horror story about fed-up birds taking it out on humanity. In a famous scene, Tippi Hedren, as good an actress as Grace Kelly at half the price, hides from murderous seagulls in a phone booth.

[24] *High Anxiety*-Mel Brooks's 1977 spoof of Hitchock films reprises a scene from *The Birds*, only in the Brooks's version, the attackers are pigeons and their weapon of choice is poop.

[25] *Duck Soup*-the 1933 madcap Marx Brothers film. In one scene, Groucho whispers conspiratorially into the ear of Ambassador Trentino, "Don't look now, but there's one man

too many in this room, and I think it's you." You've never seen *Duck Soup*? Where have you been?

[26] *Catch 22*-a brilliant 1970 film version of Joseph Heller's book of the same name about a World War II pilot obsessed with the fear that he will be the last person killed in the war, a death he considers the most pointless of all. Alan Arkin, no longer trying to kill a blind Audrey Hepburn as in the 1967 movie, *Wait Until Dark*, plays the lead role.

[27] *Laudato Si*-Pope Francis's 2015 marvelous encyclical letter "On Care for Our Common Home." Check it out at: www.vatican.va/content/francesco/en/encyclicals/documents/ papa-francesco_20150524_enciclica-laudato-si.html. (I'll give anyone a dollar who can recite the link back to me by memory.)

[28] *Repo Man*-Harry Dean Stanton and Emilio Estevez star in this 1984 zany cult classic about the men who repossess cars. In one scene, Tracy Walter as Miller says to Estevez:

> A lot o' people don't realize what's really going on. They
> view life as a bunch o' unconnected incidents 'n things. They
> don't realize that there's this, like, lattice o' coincidence that
> lays on top o' everything. Give you an example; show you
> what I mean: suppose you're thinkin' about a plate o' shrimp.
> Suddenly someone'll say, like, plate, or shrimp, or plate o'
> shrimp out of the blue, no explanation. No point in lookin'
> for one, either. It's all part of a cosmic unconciousness.

Estevez asks, "You eat a lot of acid, Miller, back in the hippie days?"

[29] *Young Frankenstein*-Mel Brooks's 1974 satire of 1930s horror movies may be his best film. Gene Hackman's cameo as a blind hermit is priceless.

[30] *The Truman Show*-a disturbing 1998 comedy starring Jim Carrey as a man who is unaware that his entire life is a televised and scripted reality show

[31] *The Matrix*-a 1999 shoot-'em-up sci fi, starring Keanu Reeves, about a rebellion against parasitic aliens who delude human beings into believing they live normal lives on earth when in reality they are prisoners. It grossed more than 463 million dollars and inspired two high school seniors, dressed like Reeves's character, to shoot thirty-three people, killing twelve, in Columbine, Colorado.

[32] *Dark City*-a 1998 sci-fi film about humans trapped on a sunless planet. They are implanted each day with fake film noir memories of life on earth. Although it never became a franchise like *The Matrix,* many critics, including me, consider it a much better film that makes a similar point without a bloodbath.

[33] *Stranger Than Fiction*-a clever, heartwarming 2006 comedy/love story starring Will Ferrell, Maggie Gyllenhaal, Emma Thompson, Dustin Hoffman, and Queen Latifah. Buster (a.k.a Tony Hale) from *Arrested Development* has a nice part, too, in one of my favorite films.

[34] *Monty Python and the Holy Grail*-a 1975 zany interpretation of the King Arthur legend. It includes a scene when clouds part and a bearded God appears, among many other unexpected and unexplained things.

[35] *deus ex machina*-according to Google:

> This Latin phrase originally described an ancient plot device used in Greek and Roman theatre. Many tragedy writers used Deus ex Machina to resolve complicated or

even seemingly hopeless situations in the plots of their plays. The phrase is loosely translated as "god from the machine."

I believe *deus ex machina* represents the most artistically lazy technique a writer can employ. When it occurs in a movie or play, audiences should demand their money back.

[36]*The Adventures of Tom Sawyer*-Mark Twain (aka Samuel Clemens) wrote the American classic in 1876 but went on to include the main character in three other novels, including *Tom Sawyer, Detective* in 1896. Although the 1896 novel is lesser known, I would be remiss in my duty as a fledgling mystery writer not to encourage you to read it. Twain initially saw Tom as a composite of three people he had known but later claimed the character emerged entirely from his fertile imagination. Although you may think Mr. Red Hand is entirely fictional, I am less and less sure about that myself.

[37]*The Murders in the Rue Morgue*-Edgar Allen Poe's short story that invented the detective murder mystery genre. Without this story, we'd never have had Sherlock Holmes, Hercule Poirot, Miss Marple, Columbo, and a me in the truer-than-fact classic, *The Man Who Cannot Be Killed*.

[38]*Murder on Mott Street: a Catholic Worker Mystery*-Never heard of it? Proceed directly to: www.scottschaefferduffy-books.com. Do not pass Go. Do not collect $200.

[39]*Midsomer Murders*-a British television detective drama depicting at least three murders per episode since 1997, racking up a body count of at least 363 and counting. Amazingly, two unarmed detectives apprehend every single murderer, no matter how dangerous. Anthony Horowitz and the original producers, Betty Willingale and Brian True-May, created the series. Horowitz adapted the majority of early

episodes from original works by Caroline Graham. Horowitz went on to write many of the best segments of the excellent British series *Foyle's War* as well as the book my daughter Grace gave me, *Magpie Murders*.

[40]*Black Mass*-a 2015 movie about the Boston mobster Whitey Bulger. Benedict Cumberbatch tries to portray Whitey's brother Billy, once president of the state senate. To watch a hysterical send-up of Cumberbatch, look up "Boston Accent Trailer-Late Night with Seth Myers-YouTube." Trust me. You won't regret it.

[41]*The Simpsons*-a comedic and satirical cartoon created for television by Matt Groening in 1989. Some say the quality has declined over the years, but, as Bart Simpson said so well in 1982 when he heard that Bill Cosby (before his ignominious fall) wanted his show to end on a high point, "Screw that! If I had a TV show, I'd drive that sucker into the ground."

[42]*American Hustle*-a 2013 gem of a movie filmed in Worcester, or as those in-the-know call it, "Paris on the Blackstone"

[43]*Boyfriend in the Car*-a campfire classic, or trope, in all its iterations. Many versions are available online.

[44]"The Hook"-another story best told in the dark and introduced with: "This is a true story. It happened in 19?? in ?? It was in all the papers." You can fill in whatever year and state you like.

[45]Morlocks-Google will tell you they are a fictional species created by H. G. Wells for his novel *The Time Machine*, but Marvel comics holds that they're outcasts living in

underground tunnels beneath New York, New Jersey, and Connecticut. I favor the latter theory.

[46]*The Screwtape Letters*-a book by C. S. Lewis, released in 1942, cleverly collects a correspondence between a demon named Screwtape and his nephew, a junior temptor named Wormwood. In one letter, Screwtape writes, "A moderated religion is as good for us as no religion at all—and more amusing."

[47]Harry Potter-a young wizard in a series of books by J. K. Rowling that began in 1997 then got made into movies and have spawned Broadway plays. *Harry Potter* catapulted Rowling from poverty into extreme wealth. She was the first author to achieve billionaire status, but, after giving much of her wealth to charity, she now makes ends meet as a millionaire.

[48]The Avengers-a team of superheroes created by Marvel Comics in 1963 and featured in the first of many movies in 2012. In case you don't know, The Avengers are: Ant-Man, the Hulk, Iron Man, Thor, the Wasp, and Captain America. Hawkeye and Black Widow came on board in the first film. Lately, they also partner with The Guardians of the Galaxy and Black Panther. Generally, Loki, Thor's ripped-off half brother, is a villain but, more and more often, he too pitches in to save the universe. Don't worry if you're confused. That's only natural.

[49]Insane Clown Posse-a horrorcore (a real word; I kid you not) hip hop duo composed of Violent J (Joseph Bruce) and Shaggy 2 Dope (Joseph Utsler) that performs in terrifying clown make-up. They have hyper-enthusiastic fans called Juggalos. For reasons I don't understand, the band and fans

elicit incredibly negative comments online, reminding me of the ire lovers of rock n' roll had toward disco in the 1970s.

[50] *Chariots of Fire*-the 1981 film about British sprinters at the 1924 Olympics opens with a pack of Brits running in their modest underwear through the no-doubt frigid English surf. For some reason, the director decided the scene should be in slow motion. Race organizers play the theme song at many races, including near the finish of the 2013 Bridge of Flowers 10K in Shelburne Falls, where I defeated Vin Garofoli to win the age group and strangest award of my career. If you come by for a visit, I'll show it to you.

[51] *Hogan's Heroes*-a very unlikely television comedy about a prisoner of war camp in Nazi Germany. While it's surprising that the show ran from 1965 until 1971, it's even more surprising it ever debuted. The prisoners refer to solitary confinement as "the cooler."

[52] *Happy Days*-a television sitcom set in the 1950s. It down-plays the McCarthy era, the nuclear threat, the Korean War, Jim Crow racism, and the struggle for civil rights to create an image of early rock 'n' roll joy.

[53] *Frog and Toad Are Friends*-an award-winning 1970 children's book by Arnold Lobel that every parent should read to their children. The cartoon version of it captures all the magic. Forty-six years after its premier, the film delights my grandchildren.

[54] *The Terminator*-the 1984 sci-fi film starring Arnold Schwarzenegger as a killer robot from the future. Directed by James Cameron, who thirteen years later would win an Academy Award for Titanic. If anyone had told me in '84 that the Schwarzenegger would go on to become governor of California,

I would have laughed. But when he-who-shall-not-be-named got elected president, unimaginable possibilities seem endless.

[55]"Luke, I am your father"-a popular misquote from George Lucas's 1977 mega sci-fi hit *Star Wars*. James Earl Jones actually says, "No, I am your father" just before Luke Skywalker starts screaming "NO!" over and over, a reaction that many people have after getting tangled up with ancesterydna.com.

[56]James Earl Jones's Sprint Facebook commercial-Do yourself a favor and Google this 2014 ad to laugh your head off at Jones and Malcolm McDowell satirizing today's computer messaging.

[57]*The Ten Commandments*-a 1956 film portrayal of the Exodus story. Yul Brynner plays Egypt's King Ramses with an impressive bass voice that sound very kingly, and Charlton Heston plays Moses.

[58]*The Little Rascals*-a 1922-1944 series of short movies collectively called Our Gang featuring the adventures of children in a poor American neighborhood. The kids are mighty independent and creative. My children confused them with The Three Stooges and called them The Three Little Rascals.

[59]*Magpie Murders*-a clever 2017 mystery wrapped around another mystery by Anthony Horowitz. It's a tip of the hat to the genre.

[60]MyPillow-an as-seen-on-TV, made-in-America product as ubiquitous as clap-on lights in the early 1970s and the Snuggie of 2012. As with all such genius inventions, a long list of complaints thrive online. Karen Pajer's husband says he bought them and they're just like any other pillow, except more expensive.

[61]*Sandman*-Although a 2017 film of this name depicts a terrible monster, I refer to the kindly character from Swedish

folklore who sprinkles magic sand onto our eyes to help us enjoy restful sleep filled with happy dreams.

[62] *Simon Birch*-a wonderful 1998 film based on John Irving's book *A Prayer for Owen Meany*. The star, Ian Smith, steals the show.

[63] *Memnoch the Devil*-a 1995 novel by Anne Rice. The devil escorts a vampire through hell and heaven to make a case against God. It's a bit like Dante's *Inferno*, only easier to read. I liked this line: "Oh, but when love is reached through suffering, it has a power it can never gain through innocence."

[64] *Jaws*-Steven Spielberg's 1975 giant shark classic film. When I first saw it in a crowded theater, everyone screamed when a severed human leg with the foot in a sneaker drifted down to the water's bottom. Everyone, that is, save a teen behind me who quoted the opening line from the TV show T*he Six-Million-Dollar Man*: "We can rebuild him. We can make him better."

[65] Blue Öyster Cult-an American rock band that came together in 1967 and recorded, among other things, "(Don't Fear) the reaper." It pains me to have to explain that Blue Öyster Cult is a band. I feel like Jack Black in School of Rock when he realizes his students have never heard of Led Zeppelin, Black Sabbath, or AC/DC and screams, "Aaah! What are they teaching in this place?"

[66] Colin Kaepernick-quarterback for the San Francisco 49ers football team who, in 2016, refused to stand for the US national anthem to protest racial injustice. As a number of NFL players, mostly black but some not, followed his lead, virulent opposition from President Trump and others led the NFL to require all players to stand for the national anthem or remain in the locker room during its performance. Kaepernick left the 49ers in 2016

and as of September, 2018, had not been signed. Amnesty International gave him its 2018 Ambassador of Conscience award. Regarding his protest, he said,

> There's a lot of racism disguised as patriotism in this country. And people don't like to address that. And they don't like to address what the root of this protest is. People want to take everything back to the flag, but that's not what we're talking about. We're talking racial discrimination, inequalities and injustices that are happening across the nation.

[67]heat merchant-a phrase the *Urban Dictionary* defines as "a person who picks on others verbally by mocking and making jokes at their expense .... Someone who brings the heat." Shakespeare loved to include heat merchants in his plays. Iago is one in *Othello*. In the first scene of *Richard III*, the Duke of Gloucester establishes himself as another when he says:

> ... since I cannot prove a lover, ... I am determined to prove a villain and hate the idle pleasures of those days. Plots have I laid, inductions dangerous, by drunken prophecies, libels and dreams, to set my brother Clarence and the king in deadly hate the one against the other.

Like Gloucester, a heat merchant is "false and treacherous.

[68]Scrubadub-a self-described "Great Carwash" that dispenses tokens accepted by the business's vacuum cleaners. For some unexplained reason, the Worcester franchise has a Bart Simpson doll strapped to the wall inside the soapy part of the carwash.

[69]Chuck E. Cheese-a so-called "family entertainment center," formerly known as Chuck E. Cheese's Pizza Time Theatre, which dispenses tokens to pay for rides and games.

In actuality, it's a high-priced parental torture center. Not that I have a strong opinion.

[70] *The Brothers Karamazov*-Fyodor Dostoevsky's final novel, which took him two years to write, was published as a serial in *The Russian Messenger* in 1879 and 1880, the same year Dostoevsky died. *Wikipedia* calls it

> a spiritual drama of moral struggles concerning faith, doubt, judgment, and reason set against a modernizing Russia, with a plot which revolves around the subject of patricide.

It was a favorite of Dorothy Day, the cofounder of the Catholic Worker movement. It may no longer be a best seller, but I think it's still something everyone should read.

[71] *Mit Brennender Sorge* (*With Burning Concern*)-Pope Pius XI's 1937 anti-Nazi encyclical smuggled into Germany. On Passion Sunday, Catholic priests read the encyclical from all Catholic pulpits. The following day, the Gestapo confiscated every copy it could find and closed all the printing presses that published it. Among other things, the letter condemned the notion of racial superiority and praised the Hebrew scriptures. Pius wrote,

> None but superficial minds could stumble into concepts of a national God, of a national religion; or attempt to lock within the frontiers of a single people, within the narrow limits of a single race, God, the Creator of the universe.

[72] *The Long Loneliness*-the 1952 autobiography of the Catholic Worker movement's cofounder, Dorothy Day. In it, she says,

> We have all known the long loneliness, and we have learned that the only solution is love and that love comes with community.

My wife Claire and I ran the 2014 Boston Marathon in shirts that proclaimed,

> The only solution is love.
>
> —Dorothy Day

[73] *Time Bandits*-Terry Gilliam's 1981 adventure/comedy about a gang of dwarf thieves who take a young British boy with them into the past as God and the devil pursue them. A weirdly enjoyable film.

[74] *Bloody Sunday*-a 2002 dramatization of the 1972 civil rights march in Derry, Northern Ireland

[75] *Millions*-a 2004 comedy/drama about money, family, and hope. Four out of five stars

[76] *The Way*-a 2010 film by Emilio Estevez starring his father, Martin Sheen, about a group of people on pilgrimage from France to Spain. A gem.

[77] *The Hobbit: an Unexpected Journey*-a 2012 version of J. R. R. Tolkien's 1937 novel. Not bad, if a bit overlong.

[78] The Great Stink of 1858-an olfactory nightmare that occurred when hot weather exacerbated the smell of untreated human waste and industrial pollutants on the banks of London's River Thames. The smell grew so foul that the curtains in Parliament were doused in bleach to obscure it.

[79] Franz Jägerstätter-an Austrian peasant, husband, and father of three girls who, as a Roman Catholic, refused to be inducted into the German Army during World War II and was beheaded by the Nazis in 1943.

[80] *Singin' in the Rain*-the 1952 film where Gene Kelly does a wonderfully cheerful dance on a soaking wet sound stage

[81]*Animal House*-National Lampoon's 1978 college fraternity send-up set at the fictional school Faber College, whose motto is "Knowledge is good"

[82]*Marshall*-a 2017 dramatization of a historic trial starring Chadwick Boseman, who is also the star of the 2018 film *Black Panther*, which may or may not be true because his highly-advanced African homeland, Wakanda, uses high-tech methods to hide itself from the outside world

[83]*Downsizing*-a 2017 social satire starring Matt Damon and having more to say than I expected

[84]ants on a burning log-a analogy with the inevitability of death from Ernest Hemingway's 1929 novel of the Spanish Civil War, *A Farewell to Arm*s

[85]*Tremors*-a bizarre 1990 American movie about giant monsters that live underground and attack when they sense motion or sound on the surface

[86]graboids-the name Victor Wong gave for subterranean giant monsters in the six *Tremors* movies. According to UGO. com, "Graboids are to the desert what sharks are to the ocean." As if we didn't have enough to worry about after *Sharknado*.

[87]*Miracle on Thirty-fourth Street*-a 1947 classic about Santa working in a New York City department store

[88]*The Polar Express*-a kind of creepy 2004 movie loosely based on Chris Van Allsburg's 1985 children's book about a train that takes children to see Santa at the North Pole

[89]*Silver Linings Playbook*-a 2012 comedy/drama/love story classic film

[90]*Farewell to Arms*-Ernest Hemingway's 1929 bummer

[91]*Annie Hall*-Woody Allen's 1977 classic comedy/love story. I hesitate to mention his films after Allen ditched his wife

Mia Farrow, married their adopted daughter, and was accused of sexual misconduct by his son.

[92] *What Men Live By*-Leo Tolstoy's 1885 masterpiece short story about an angel sentenced to stay on earth for refusing God's command to take the life of a mother who has just delivered twins. A must read, trust me.

[93] *Mork and Mindy*-a television sitcom about an affable alien that ran from 1978 until 1982

[94] *Small Is Beautiful: A Study of Economics as if People Mattered*- a 1973 collection of essays by the economist E. F. Schumacher. The *New York Times Literary Supplement* ranked it among the hundred most influential books published since World War II.

[95] "Eat, drink, and be merry, for tomorrow we die."-Ecclesiastes 8:15

[96] *The Blair Witch Project*-a 1999 horror mystery, purported to be comprised of documentary footage left behind by missing college students

[97] *Angel Heart*-a terrifying and clever 1987 murder mystery that will shock you

[98] *The Devil's Advocate*-a 1997 horror movie with a great take on Satan's false promises

[99] *Legend*-a 1985 horror fantasy with an old-fashioned devil complete with horns, tail, and bright red skin.

[100] *The Witches of Eastwick*-a 1987 horror film based on a novel by John Updike. Jack Nicholson ramps up his diabolical side in the last third.

[101] *The Prophecy*-a 1995 horror film about a not-cool and grim tussle for the soul of a little girl

[102]*Bedazzled*-a comic horror movie. Lucifer takes on the form of a sexy woman to dupe Brendan Fraser.

[103]*South Park*-a satirical cartoon comedy show that began in 1997. In one episode, Satan says, "Without evil there could be no good, so it must be good to be evil sometimes." In another, he loses a boxing match with Jesus. On this show, anything goes.

[104]*Oh, God*-a 1977 comedy. God recruits a grocery store manager, played by John Denver, as his apostle. George Burns portrays an affable but not impressive God. In the 2003 comedy *Bruce Almighty*, Morgan Freeman has my vote for the best film deity. After Jim Carrey complains, "God is a mean kid sitting on an ant hill with a magnifying glass . . . He could fix my life in five minutes, but he'd rather burn off my feelers and watch me squirm," Freeman teaches him a good lesson. When Carrey asks, "God takes vacations?" Freeman replies breezily, "Sure. Haven't you heard of the Dark Ages?"

[105]" . . . if I talk about God, my record won't get played"- lyrics from hip hop artist Kanye West's song "Jesus Walks"

[106]*Spy Kids II:Island of Lost Dreams*-"Island of Lost Plots" would be more accurate. You now know the best line of the entire 2003 comedy/adventure.

[107]*Harvey*-a whimsical 1950 comedy. Jimmy Stewart has a friendship with an imaginary six-foot tall rabbit. I liked this film almost as much as *A Thousand Clowns*, a 1965 master-piece with Jason Robards, who says, "If things aren't funny, then they're exactly what they are; and then they're like a long dental appointment."

[108]"a stranger on a bus"-from Joan Osborne's 1995 song when she asks, "If God had a name, what would it be?" and poses the question

> What if God was one of us
> just a slob like one of us
> just a stranger on the bus
> trying to make His way home?

[109] *Silence*-Shusaku Endo's 1966 novel of historical fiction about a Jesuit missionary in seventeenth-century Japan who wrestles with the idea of God's silence during persecution of believers.

colophon

Text for *The Man Who Cannot Be Killed* is set in Adobe Caslon Pro. Caslon is the name given to serif typefaces designed by William Caslon I (c. 1692–1766) in London or inspired by his work.

Caslon worked as an engraver of punches, the masters used to stamp the moulds or matrices used to cast metal type. He worked in the tradition of what is now called old-style serif letter design,that produced letters with a relatively organic structure resembling handwriting with a pen. Caslon established a tradition of engraving type in London, which previously had not been common. His typefaces established a strong reputation for their quality and their attractive appearance, suitable for extended passages of text.

Caslon's typefaces were popular in his lifetime and beyond, and after a brief period of eclipse in the early nineteenth century, they returned to popularity, particularly for setting printed body text and books. Many revivals exist, with varying faithfulness to Caslon's original design. Modern Caslon revivals also often add features such as a matching boldface.

Titles for *The Man Who Cannot Be Killed* are sent in Bodoni, the name given to the serif typefaces first designed by Giambattista Bodoni (1740–1813) in the late eighteenth century and frequently revived since. Bodoni's typefaces are classified as didone or modern. Bodoni followed the ideas of John Baskerville, as found in the printing type Baskerville but he took them to a more extreme conclusion.

Bodoni had a long career, and his designs changed and varied, ending with a typeface of a slightly condensed underlying structure.

When first released, Bodoni and other didone fonts were called classical designs because of their rational structure. They came to be called modern serif fonts and then, until the mid twentieth century, they were known as didone designs. Bodoni's later designs are rightfully called modern, but the earlier designs are now called transitional.